LET'S GET FESTIVE!

Celebrations Around
the World

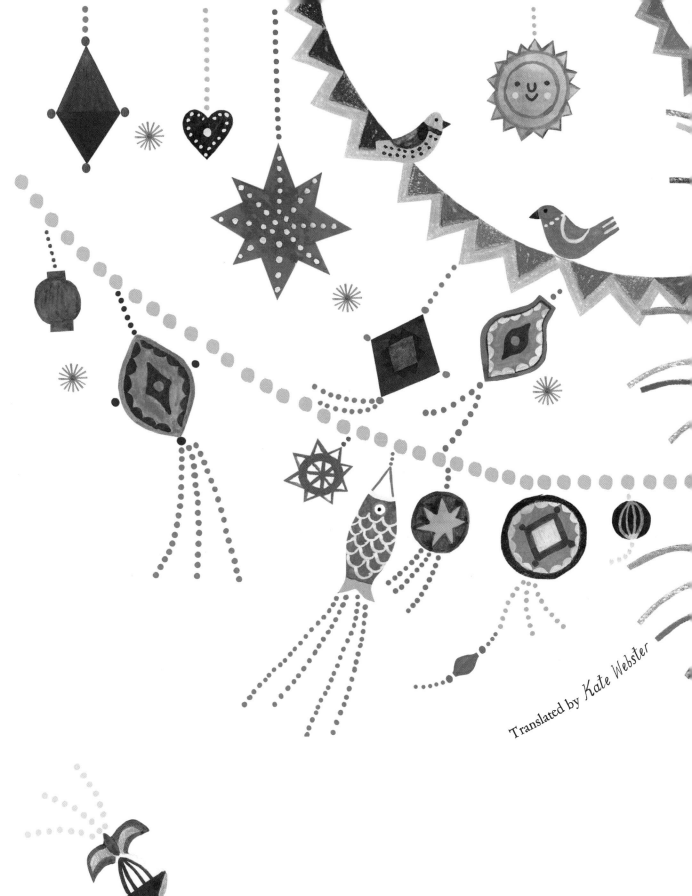

Translated by *Kate Webster*

Joanna Kończak

Ewa Poklewska-Koziełło

LET'S GET FESTIVE !

Celebrations Around the World

North South

Contents

Introduction

Do you like celebrations? I won't be surprised if you say yes. During the holidays, we get to take a break from our usual routine, and things like family meals become special and festive. So let's find out about some of the holidays and festivals that are celebrated around the world. As you'll see, while they're quite diverse, they also have a lot in common. Because in fact, no matter where, why, or how they are celebrated, holidays are usually about the same thing: community and coming together. Instead of exploring them chronologically (many have changeable dates), we'll explore them by theme: ways of welcoming the new year, holidays related to natural phenomena, important religious celebrations, joyful carnivals, remembering loved ones who have died, commemorating historical events, and other special occasions.

When we think of holidays, we often think of tradition. A tradition is something that has been practiced for a long time, deeply rooted in the customs of a country or a particular ethnic or religious group. But how we mark these special occasions hasn't remained the same over time. Traditions can change, intertwine, be imposed or fought against, and be replaced by other traditions, and "a long time" can mean a few dozen, a few hundred, or even a few thousand years. For example, the first Christians would have been very surprised at the sight of a Christmas tree or Santa Claus . . . in fact, the very celebration of Christmas itself would have surprised them! Sometimes, old customs disappear or lose their original meaning and new ones emerge in their place. When I was growing up in Poland, I only knew about Halloween from foreign movies. These days, come fall, I'm often found handing out candy to trick-or-treating kids and carving pumpkins. My grandma used to tell me about Christmas carolers who would come to the house carrying a star and dressed as barnyard animals, but I never saw them myself. It's interesting to note these changes.

If you want to know more about the holidays in this book, you might not have to travel far. Maybe you have neighbors or friends who celebrate them. I've participated in various celebrations, both on trips abroad and in my own hometown. Even in Poland, where I live, there are celebrations to mark Durga Puja and Chinese New Year, organized by representatives of the communities, cultural centers, and museums. Often, the celebrations also showcase the music, dance, or cuisine of the particular country or community. Search for interesting events online with your grown-ups and find out how you can join in the celebrations!

Joanna Kończak

New Year's Eve and New Year's Day

On the night of December 31, we bid farewell to the old year and greet the new one. For many people, this is a special evening: an occasion for celebration.

Grand balls, parties, and outdoor events are held all around the world. People gather in city squares and on beaches to dance, party with friends, and wait for the stroke of midnight to mark the end of one year and the beginning of the next. As midnight arrives, the sky is lit up with fireworks or laser shows, and people make wishes and resolutions.

Midnight arrives at different moments, depending on where you are in the world. The first people to welcome the new year are the residents of Kiribati and the islands of Samoa and Tonga. People in New York City are just waking up at that time. The very last to celebrate are the residents of Hawaii.

The custom of celebrating the new year has been present in many cultures since ancient times, but its location on the calendar has changed. In ancient Rome, the celebrations originally took place in spring before moving to January 1. Although the exact year the dates changed is unknown, in 46 BCE Julius Caesar reformed the Roman lunar calendar, which officially marked the beginning of the new year on January 1 and it hasn't changed since. The need to adjust the Roman calendar was because of a mismatch between the date system and the seasons, with the dates for December falling in what was actually September. To deal with this change, the year 46 BCE was extended by eighty days, so it lasted 445 days in total. In Latin, it was known as *annus confusionis*: "the year of confusion."

The new calendar was called the Julian calendar, and it is still used in the Orthodox Church today. But in 1582 CE the Gregorian calendar, introduced by Pope Gregory XIII, was proposed as a way to minimize the difference between the calendar and the tropical year (defined by the moment the sun passes through a specific point), since the Julian calendar was one day late every 128 years. Not all countries adopted the Gregorian calendar in 1582, though, which has led to complications in the dating of historical events. (The current difference between the dates of the two calendars is 13 days.) So we might hear about the October Revolution in the Russian Empire, even though it took place in November according to today's Gregorian calendar. However, at that time, the Julian calendar was still in use in the Russian Empire. There is also some confusion over the dates of death of the writers William Shakespeare and Miguel de Cervantes. According to the calendars in use in 1616 in each man's country of origin, it seems they died on the same day. In fact, they died one day apart.

The Gregorian calendar is now formally used all over the world. In 2016, Saudi Arabia, which had until then officially used the Muslim lunar calendar, switched to the Gregorian system. In many places, however, other calendars related to a certain culture or religion are also recognized. In India, the Indian national calendar (a solar calendar from the Saka era) functions as the official one alongside the Gregorian.

Calendars are either linear, with the passage of time counted from a specific date, or—like the Chinese calendar—cyclical, with years passing in repeating cycles. In some countries, especially in Asia, January 1 has only administrative significance, and the new year is celebrated at a different time. In other places, there are double celebrations!

Apparently, one of the original reasons for joyfully celebrating the eve of the new year was fear that the world would end. In the year 999 CE, at the turn of the first millennium, Christians recalled the prophecies of the oracle Sibyl, which predicted that a monster called Leviathan would awaken and devour the Earth and the sky. According to legend, Leviathan had been defeated some centuries earlier and imprisoned in the dungeons of the Lateran (then the residence of the papacy) by Pope Sylvester I. Terrible visions of the end of the world were also found in the Bible's book of Revelation and were linked to the prophecies of Sibyl. To make matters worse, in the year 999 CE the Catholic Church was led by Pope Sylvester II. Rumors circulated among the terrified people that the first Sylvester had imprisoned the beast, and the second would release it. However, when the year 1000 arrived and the world did not end, people ran out of their homes full of joy and relief. The pope gave a new year's blessing "to the city and to the world," which is a religious tradition in Rome to this day.

Sylvester I, the legendary vanquisher of Leviathan, died on December 31, 335 CE. In his honor, churchgoers in Europe celebrate Saint Sylvester's Day on the eve of the new year.

The arrival of the new year was also feared not so long ago, at the end of 1999. This time around, people weren't worried about a terrible monster and an apocalypse, but about the "millennium bug." In early computers, to save memory the date was shortened to the last two digits of the year, so the machines would read the years 1901 and 2001 exactly the same. As a result, a chain of computer system failures was expected, with potentially grim consequences. However, the crisis was averted, and just as the world did not end in 1000, computers did not crash in 2000. Thankfully, now we just focus on celebrating the arrival of a new year and looking forward to what it may bring.

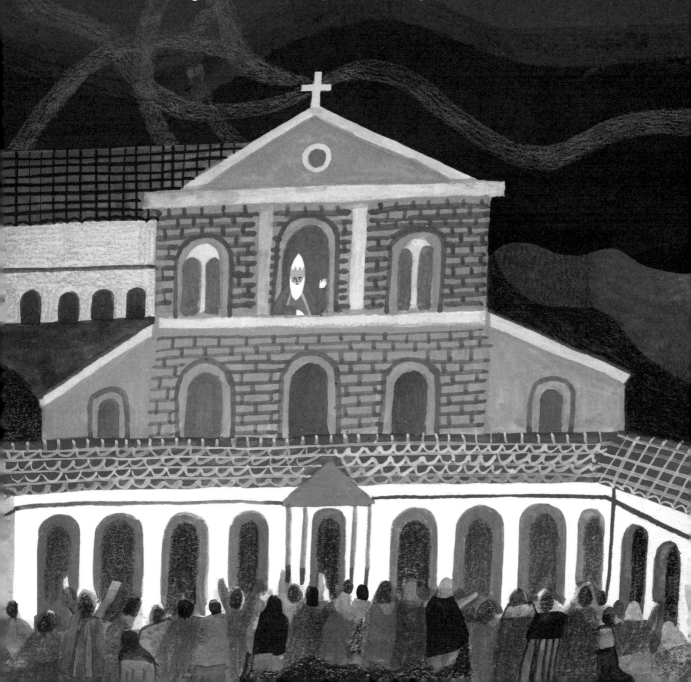

Nowruz

In ancient Persian, the word *nowruz* means "new day." The Nowruz holiday relates to both the new year and the cycle of nature, because it is celebrated in Iran with the arrival of spring, or more precisely, the spring equinox. It falls on March 20 or 21. Nowruz ends on the thirteenth day of the new year, so the celebration lasts twelve days, symbolizing the twelve months.

The traditions associated with Nowruz go back three thousand years and draw on Zoroastrianism, a religion that was widespread in the Persian Empire (it is still practiced by a small number of people in Iran and other countries). Nowadays, Nowruz is a secular holiday celebrated by people of different faiths. Because the Persian Empire extended far beyond the borders of modern Iran, the Nowruz customs, which vary regionally, are also found in other countries, including Afghanistan, Azerbaijan, and Tajikistan. The holiday is also celebrated by Kurds in Iraq and Turkey, and by Parsis in India. It is estimated that up to three hundred million people around the world celebrate Nowruz!

In Iran, preparations for Nowruz start in advance: it is tradition to thoroughly clean the entire house in order to enter the next year purely and happily. To celebrate

properly, people buy new clothes and sometimes new furniture. The first stage of bidding farewell to the old year begins on the last Wednesday before the equinox, with a festival called Chaharshanbe Suri. In the evening, people gather and light bonfires in streets and gardens, then jump over the flames. This symbolizes the cleansing power of fire as well as the victory of light over darkness. As people jump, they will sometimes shout, "*Zardee maan az toh! Sorkhee toh az maan!*" which translates to: "My yellow is yours, your red is mine." (Traditionally in Persian culture, yellow is the color

of disease and red is the color of health.) Fireworks are lit as well. The dancing, singing, and fun continue late into the night. There is also a custom known as *ghashogh-zani* ("spoon banging") that resembles Halloween trick-or-treating. Children and young people wrap themselves in veils and go from house to house in the neighborhood. They bang spoons on pots and pans and ask for treats. The spoon banging is meant to banish all the bad luck of the past year. It also symbolizes visits from the spirits of the dead.

Nowruz is a time to meet with family and neighbors, feasting together and strengthening friendships. Many people go to visit elderly relatives. Grandparents hand out nuts and candy, and children receive small gifts. An important part of the celebrations is the preparation of the festive table called *haftsin*. It must contain seven things—seven is a lucky number in Iran—starting with the letter *S* in Persian. The items include: *sabzeh*, sprouts of barley, wheat, or cress, symbolizing rebirth; *sir*, garlic, representing medicine and health; *sib*, apple, meaning beauty; *samanu*, a sweet pudding made of wheat germ and flour, symbolizing fertility and harvest; *serkeh*, vinegar, meaning patience; *sekke*, coins, intended to bring prosperity; *sonbol*, hyacinth, embodying spring; *sendjed*, olives, representing love; and *sumac*, a spice obtained from the purple fruit of a shrub, signifying sunrise.

The table might also be decorated with a mirror, a candlestick, a pomegranate, eggs with painted shells, or a goldfish in a bowl. Some people add a copy of the Quran, the holy book of Islam, with paper money between the pages for the children; or Ferdowsi's *Shahnameh* (a Persian national epic); or a collection of poetry by Hafez. The exact selection of items on the Nowruz table depends on the specific home and family traditions.

On the thirteenth day of Nowruz, Sizdah Bedar, everyone goes outside for a picnic. People make wishes and return the sprouted greens from the Nowruz table to nature by throwing them into a stream. This is a symbolic send-off of all misfortunes. Young people who want to find a partner tie the stalks of the greens together. On this day, Iranians also play tricks as part of the tradition of *Dorugh-e Sizdah*, "Lie of the Thirteenth," similar to April Fool's Day.

What do people eat during this holiday? Apart from dried fruits and nuts, there are omelets with lots of herbs called *kuku sabzi* and, of course, baklava and other sweet dishes.

Chinese New Year

This holiday is associated with the legend of the demon Nian, who would sneak into villages and harass people and animals. However, when people discovered that the monster was afraid of noise and the color red, they dressed up in red costumes and made loud noises in whatever way they could. The terrified creature fled, causing an outburst of joy, which is the key feature of the celebration to this day. Firecrackers are used to symbolically scare away evil spirits, and the auspicious color of red is an intrinsic part of New Year celebrations.

The holiday, also called the Spring Festival or Lunar New Year, is celebrated in various countries in East and Southeast Asia, including Taiwan, Singapore, Malaysia, and other places where there is a large Chinese community, and lasts around two weeks. At this time of the year in these regions, the weather can cause problems—in the form of either drought or flood—so various rituals were historically used to ensure prosperity. Another important part of the tradition is to take a break after working hard all year. There are specific customs and dishes associated with the celebrations depending on the place. For example, in Vietnam, where New Year is called Tết, people serve *bánh chưng*, a slow-cooked dish of glutinous rice, pork, and mung beans wrapped in *dong* leaves.

Chinese New Year falls between the end of January and the end of February of the Gregorian calendar, with the exact date determined according to the Chinese luni-solar calendar, which was once used for agricultural purposes. Each year is described by one of the five elements (metal, earth, fire, water, wood) and one of the twelve animals of the Chinese zodiac (dog, pig, rat, ox, tiger, rabbit, dragon, snake, horse, goat, monkey, rooster). The features of the patron animal are supposed to influence what the year will be like.

Families want to spend New Year together, and since they can be scattered all over China (and around the world), it is estimated that this occasion is one of the largest migrations of people on a global scale. Every year, millions of people embark on a New Year's journey. Students return home, and adult children visit their parents. This is not a good time to plan other trips: trains, planes, and buses are hugely overcrowded and significantly more expensive than at other times of the year. There is even a specific word in Chinese to describe the intense travel rush around New Year: *chūnyùn*.

Everything stops for almost two weeks. Factories arrange their production cycles so that they can take a longer break during this time. Service centers, institutions, and many shops are closed. Anyone doing business with someone from China must take into account that they won't hear from them for some time.

For some people, the holiday is their only chance in the year to see their loved ones. Getting together for meals is an extremely important element of this celebration. Families are reunited, old friendships are strengthened, and new ones are made. Streets, parks, shops, and restaurants are full of New Year decorations: lanterns, flowers, images of the animal patron of the coming year, and plenty of red,

the traditional color of happiness and prosperity. Houses are decorated with cutouts or New Year pictures called *niánhùa*. They can have various themes and might depict scenes from everyday life, deities, auspicious animals, historical events, or myths. They are supposed to provide year-round protection. People hang poems written in beautiful calligraphy on their doors, which is also a way to show off their sophistication.

There are various dos and don'ts associated with the holiday season. You should not enter the new year with unsettled debts. Superstitious people will not cut their hair in the first month of the new year, believing it could cause the death of a family

member. This means that hairdressers are extremely busy before the holidays. As part of New Year preparations, houses are carefully tidied, but after the arrival of the new year, there is no sweeping for the first two days to avoid mistakenly brushing away prosperity and wealth. For similar reasons, people refrain from pouring out water and taking out the garbage, which can make laundry and doing the dishes a little tricky. In the past, people would pour dirty dish water into buckets or bowls, which were emptied later, but nowadays, especially in cities, people no longer make such sacrifices.

On Chinese New Year's Eve, family and friends gather for a celebratory dinner. Dressed in their best clothes, they stay up late talking, playing games, and watching TV. People used to stay awake all night long, but now it's usually only until midnight, when firecrackers and fireworks are lit. This noisy custom isn't practiced everywhere anymore: various cities and regions prohibit it due to excessive environmental pollution and fire hazards resulting from the densely packed buildings.

During this holiday, it is important to remember and honor deceased ancestors by burning incense on the home altar and leaving out offerings of fruit and different foods. Paper money is also burned for the ancestors to use in the afterlife. It is believed that well-tended ancestors take care of the family, guaranteeing their prosperity and safety. Good wishes are also expressed: first to the elders, then to other relatives, and finally to neighbors and friends.

Each day of the celebration has its own customs (often slightly different depending on the region). For example, on one day people invite the god of money into their homes, hoping to win his favor. On that day it is customary to serve various dishes with names that have the same pronunciation as words related to fortune and prosperity.

Children receive red envelopes with money from their grandparents, which is a centuries-old tradition. Before they receive

this gift, the children must make a deep, respectful bow to their elders. Other people in the family might also receive envelopes. Nowadays, some people send red envelopes online.

In the south of China, people perform dragon and lion dances outside Buddhist and Taoist temples and at special displays. The dragon, which is made of fabric and has a long, snake-like body, is steered by several people using sticks, performing rhythmic movements and lots of sudden turns. The dancing lion is operated by two puppeteers.

One controls the huge head and jaws (with their own legs serving as the front paws), and the other controls the hind part of the animal. The display often includes very difficult and spectacular acrobatic elements, accompanied by a hypnotic drum rhythm. The performers collect donations from the audience, delivered straight into the lion's mouth!

The culmination of the Chinese New Year celebration is the Lantern Festival, when people light lanterns, write New Year wishes, and eat *yuánxiāo* or *tāngyuán* dumplings made of glutinous rice flour with a sweet filling.

There are many festive dishes, and as you already know, different regions have their own customs and specialties. In the north of China, the festive table will usually feature steamed *jiǎozi* dumplings stuffed with vegetables, meat, or seafood. Some people hide dried fruits or a coin in one of the dumplings. The person who finds it is expected to enjoy exceptional prosperity in the new year. In the south, where rice is preferred, people make glutinous rice cakes. How fortunate—not only is the food delicious, but it brings luck as well!

Songkran

Another way to celebrate New Year is with a splash! In Thailand, water plays a central role in the festivities. Nowadays, this holiday is celebrated on April 13 and the days that follow.

Usually, Songkran lasts until April 15, but sometimes the government extends the holiday period to make it easier for people to travel to visit family. The name comes from Sanskrit and means "passing" or "approaching." It refers to the movement of the sun between the positions on the zodiac, or the constellations. Although there are several of these transitions during the year, in this case it relates to the time when the sun moves into Aries and the cycle of the Buddhist calendar begins anew. Sanskrit is an ancient Indian language, which, like ancient Greek or Latin, is now thought to be dead, meaning no one speaks it on a daily basis. So how come this Indian language is

used for the name of a Thai holiday? Well, Indian culture once had a great influence in Thailand that is still visible today.

One of the important parts of Songkran celebrations involves visiting a Buddhist temple and offering food to the monks. People also bring other gifts, such as sand that can be used for reconstruction and repairs. Statues of the Buddha are washed with water, which symbolizes the cleansing of sins and driving away bad luck. Sometimes, to heighten the festive atmosphere, people wear colorful traditional clothing. Young people wash the hands of older family members as a sign of respect. Tributes are also paid to deceased loved ones by burning candles on the altar and leaving fruit and drinks as offerings.

After the cleaning of the statues, the people are next in line: a great water fight ensues. Sometimes, entire streets are closed to traffic to provide a safe arena for the battles. Tourists are also eager to join in the fun. At roadside stalls, you can buy water guns and buckets filled with water.

Fire pumps are made available to add to the fun, and shopkeepers and residents put out barrels of water so that people don't run out of supplies. Even staying in your car doesn't guarantee you'll keep dry. Roads are often blocked by groups of revelers who won't allow cars to pass until the driver lowers the windows. In that way, everyone complies with the custom.

In case you're concerned that a water-based celebration will end with everyone getting hypothermia, bear in mind that April in Thailand is dry and very hot. Since temperatures can reach 104 degrees Fahrenheit (40 degrees Celsius), a water fight can actually provide some respite. If you ever have the opportunity to join in the celebrations, remember that certain rules apply: don't pour water on monks, elderly people, or families with small children, and don't disturb religious processions.

Rosh Hashanah

The celebration of the Jewish New Year tastes of apples and honey. It doesn't involve noise or partying, but focuses on reflection and tranquility. Its name in Hebrew literally means "head of the year." Just as the head "directs" the body, this holiday determines what the whole year will look like. It takes place on the first two days of Tishrei, a month in the Hebrew calendar, and commemorates the biblical story of the creation of the world—Adam and Eve in particular. So it is not only about the birth of the new year but also about the birth of humankind.

The holiday is marked by the solemn, piercing sound of the shofar, a ram's horn. Unless the date of the new year falls on Shabbat, a time of rest from all work, the shofar is sounded in synagogues. It is a call to repentance. For those who are religious, it is obligatory to listen to the shofar, which is blown one hundred times during the prayers on Rosh Hashanah. The sounds produced on this instrument are not random. There are four specific ones: *tekiah*, a single, long blast; *shevarim*, three medium-length sounds; *teruah*, a quick string of nine blasts; and *tekiah gedolah*, a long, moving sound.

The holiday starts at sundown the night before the first day. On the first day of Rosh Hashanah, *tashlich*, the ceremony of casting off sins, takes place. People walk along the shore or bank of a lake, sea, or river. They pray and shake dirt from their pockets or throw crumbs of bread into the water to symbolically rid themselves of their sins. The bread is intended to be food for the fish, which according to tradition are the cleanest creatures. This is because they live in water, and water symbolizes the holy book of Judaism, the Torah.

During Rosh Hashanah, people eat a celebratory feast with their families. Before the main dishes, they eat small amounts of various items, each with a symbolic meaning, that are supposed to bode well for the new year. The selection of these items depends on the location and the family. There are no bitter or sour dishes, so as not to cause bitterness and unpleasantness.

A key part of the meal for many Jews is a dish of apples dipped in honey. This symbolizes the wisdom of the Torah and is meant to ensure sweetness for the future. People also eat pomegranates, so that their good deeds will be as numerous as pomegranate seeds. The head of a fish or a lamb may also be eaten, symbolizing the importance of being at the forefront rather than at the back. This means that you should move forward and not look back at the past. Another delicacy on the New Year table is challah, an egg-rich yeast-leavened bread. It is also baked for other holidays, but the Rosh Hashanah version is round to symbolize the life cycle. It is eaten with honey, not salt, as is usual for the other holidays. Many people also eat tzimmes, a sweet dish made of carrots stewed for a long time with sugar and dried fruits.

Rosh Hashanah begins a ten-day period of repentance that lasts until the holiday of Yom Kippur. This is when Jews remember their past deeds, try to correct mistakes they have made, and make amends to the people they have wronged.

Jews believe that on the first day of the new year, God opens three books and records people's fates for the coming year according to their good and bad deeds. Those who do good are recorded in the Book of Life, sinners are recorded in the Book of Death, and those between good and evil are recorded in the third book. On Yom Kippur, the books are closed and a verdict is reached on each person's fate.

Harvest Festival

While a harvest brings pride and joy in the fruits of labor, it is also an opportunity to thank nature for its generous gifts that keep us well fed. The holidays and celebrations that focus on expressing this gratitude, or calling for a bountiful crop the following year, are called harvest festivals. They have various names in different countries, but what they share is their joyful character and respect for the fruits of the earth.

In Polish tradition, the harvest festival is called Dożynki, Obrzynki, Wyżynki (all of which relate to harvesting of the last winter grains), or Wieńczyny (named after the wreath that is an important part of the holiday). Dożynki is the end of the harvesting time, a period of intensive work, and is accompanied by rituals that, like many other customs, have lost their original meaning over time and remained mainly as popular folk activities. Historically, the holiday was held at various times between August and September, but now it usually falls after August 15, when the Feast of the Assumption is celebrated in the Christian church. It is thought that Dożynki has been celebrated in Poland since the sixteenth century. However, its origins go back much further, to pre-Christian Slavic rituals dedicated to harvest deities.

An important element of the ancient festivities was the making of a harvest wreath, usually from rye, wheat, or both. Rye and wheat are extremely important crops because they are used to make bread, the basis of everyday meals. These grains were once thought to have magical properties. Wheat was supposed to ensure a good harvest the following year. Rye was associated with the world of spirits and the dead. Sometimes it was sprinkled on a coffin so that the ghost would be too occupied with counting grain to haunt the household, and so that the grain in the field wouldn't wither like the person who had died. The wreaths were decorated with twigs of hazel and rowan. Both of these plants were believed to have magical properties. The rowan twigs were intended to ensure that the next year's grain would be as large as the rowan's fruit. People carried the wreath to church for a blessing. Then it was taken to the manor house or farmstead in a colorful procession, accompanied by joyful singing. The best female harvester carried the wreath in her hands (sometimes with someone's

help) or on her head. The wreaths were made in various shapes, usually forming a large circle or crown.

At the manor house, the wreath was ceremonially handed over to the owners of the manor and the fields, after which a feast and dance were held for the harvesters. Folk bands played into the night. The grain from the wreath was included in the first sowing, which was supposed to ensure the success of future harvests. A small tuft of unharvested ears of grain was left in the field, tied at the top with straw, and sometimes decorated with flowers and ribbons. It was called the quail. The tuft was meant to provide shelter for quails living among the grain.

Nowadays, harvest festivals often take place in agricultural areas. They are organized by local councils and are usually accompanied by fairs and other types of celebrations. The wreaths look different now too. They are large and solid—impossible to wear on your head. The wreath decoration methods have also changed, and the people who create them are extremely inventive. A loaf of bread is often placed inside. Competitions are organized for the most beautiful wreath, and winning is a big deal!

New Yam Festival

Sometimes harvest celebrations focus on one specific crop. This is the case with the yam, a tropical vine that produces edible tubers. Depending on the species, a single tuber can weigh from a few pounds to over fifty pounds. In many places, yams are an important element of the daily diet. In some West African countries, such as Ghana and Nigeria, this nutritious and delicious vegetable is celebrated with its own holiday.

The New Yam Festival falls any time between August and October, depending on when the rainy season ends. It marks the end of the previous crop cycle and the beginning of the next. But the significance of the festival is not only agricultural. It brings together local communities (it is celebrated by many ethnic groups) and is also an affirmation of life and joy. Although it was once closely associated with certain African religions (there are various stories about these vegetables being gifts from the gods), nowadays anyone can participate in the celebrations. It has become an opportunity to remember old customs and maintain a common heritage. The festival features attractions including music and singing, cheerful processions, lively dance shows, masquerades, and acrobat displays. It is celebrated not only by agricultural communities but also by people

living in cities or abroad. During the festivities, people also pay tribute to their deceased ancestors and give thanks to their god or gods.

The exact conduct of the celebrations varies depending on the region. As one of the most important elements, a stew is made from the new harvest of yams and served to the village leader or an important representative of the community, after which everyone else can eat it. It used to be forbidden to eat the new harvest before the festival, as it was thought to bring bad luck. Today, this custom is no longer strictly observed.

Holi

The Indian festival of Holi shimmers with all the colors of the rainbow. It announces the end of winter and the arrival of spring's abundance. It is also known as the Festival of Colors because the celebration involves people throwing brightly colored powders at each other! As these powders, called *gulal*, swirl in the air, the streets turn into a vibrant jumble of people laughing, dancing, and singing.

The people who gather to celebrate often join joyful processions of musicians playing trumpets and drums. Dyed water is also used to add to the colorful frenzy. On this day, if you go outside dressed in bright clothes, it might be treated as an invitation to party. Many people wear white on Holi so that the rainbow stains are even more striking. The powders and dyed water certainly leave their mark. Even a few days later, you can tell who was celebrating by the colorful streaks remaining on foreheads and behind the ears! Holi is a Hindu festival, but anyone can join in. The arrival of spring brings happiness for everyone.

It's also tradition to play with colors in the comfort of your own home, smearing the faces of loved ones to wish them a happy Holi. People eat special holiday treats, such as crispy golden *jalebi*, a fried batter sticky with sweet syrup.

The celebration takes place in the Hindu calendar month of Phalguna, on the day after the full moon (in the Gregorian calendar, this is usually at the end of February or beginning of March). It lasts two days and starts with an evening bonfire on the night of the full moon.

Holi commemorates a specific story. There was once an arrogant and powerful demon king named Hiranyakashipu. He had a deep hatred of the god Vishnu and forbade anyone to worship him. Despite the ban,

Hiranyakashipu's son, Prahlada, continued to worship Vishnu. This angered the demon king so much that he asked his sister, the demoness Holika, to kill his son. Holika had a superpower: she was invulnerable to fire. She tricked Prahlada into going into the flames. However, Prahlada did not lose faith and was saved by Vishnu, while Holika was consumed by fire.

Then Vishnu decided to deal with Hiranyakashipu. The demon king was not easy to defeat because he also had a special power: he could not be killed by any animal, human, or god, neither by day nor by night, neither outside nor inside, and not on land, nor in water or air. So Vishnu defeated him in the form of a man-lion (neither human nor animal), at dawn (at the end of night, but before daybreak), on the threshold of the palace (neither outside nor inside), with the demon king sitting on his lap (not on land, nor in water or air).

Therefore, Holi also celebrates the victory of good over evil, life over death. Images of Holika are burned in a bonfire to bid farewell to winter and death, and to welcome the new and the good.

The custom of marking the face with colors is explained by tales of the god Krishna and his beloved Radha. The story goes that the blue-skinned Krishna, while in a mischievous mood, playfully smeared color on Radha's cheeks.

Holi is celebrated primarily in northern India. During the festival, farmers pray for a good harvest in the coming months. In different parts of the country, there are other winter, spring, and fall harvest celebrations—for example, Pongal in the southeastern state of Tamil Nadu, Lohri in the northeastern state of Punjab, and Onam in the southwestern state of Kerala. Onam is accompanied by many interesting customs, such as arranging *pookalam*, flower decorations on the floor; *puli kali*, dances in tiger costumes; *vallam kali*, longboat races; tug-of-war competitions; and *sadya*, a meal consisting of a few (or sometimes several dozen) small portions of various dishes served with rice, most often on a plate made from a large banana leaf.

Hanami

In Japanese, *hanami* literally means "flower viewing." And that is exactly what this holiday involves. People in Japan love to admire the delicate pink petals blooming on the cherry trees in spring. During Hanami, they gather for picnics and enjoy feasting among the trees.

Cherry trees—*sakura* in Japanese—are planted in parks and squares, and around Buddhist temples. Hanami draws large crowds. To get a good viewing spot, you need to arrive early. Some people take the first train in the morning to secure their place. In offices where company picnics are arranged, the task of nabbing a spot will be assigned to a low-ranking employee. Various products are branded with special *sakura* packaging—for example, you can buy Coca-Cola with cherry blossoms on the label.

In the Tokyo and Kyoto regions, the cherry blossom season falls at the end of March or the start of April. Although Japan is not a large country, it is long. Different regions have different climates. So in the south, on the tropical island of Okinawa, the trees are already covered with flowers in February. In the north, in Hokkaido, the

blossoms appear in May. Every year, information is given in the news and online about the "cherry blossom front," providing predictions of the flowering times for different places. The trees look their most beautiful a week after the flowers open.

The Hanami tradition derives from very ancient times and emerged under the influence of Chinese court culture. Initially inspired by poetry, people admired the blossoms of the *ume* plum (which are also still admired today). This was a pastime for the aristocrats at first, but gradually other parts of society also began to participate. Even the samurai (elite warriors) enjoyed flower viewing. Their lives were sometimes compared to the fate of *sakura* flowers: beautiful, but brief.

If there are cherry trees in your area, come springtime you can admire their flowers yourself. In some parks and botanical gardens, entire cherry tree alleys have been planted for our enjoyment!

Kupala Night

The night of June 20 or 21 is the shortest night of the year in the northern hemisphere. This is the summer solstice, when light triumphs over darkness. The ancient Slavs associated the summer solstice with the activities of demonic forces struggling against good, like night against day. To protect themselves from these forces, they performed various rituals and love spells.

Kupala Night, also called Sobótka, was historically celebrated in Eastern Slavic villages (which includes Ukraine, Belarus, Poland, and Russia). During the festivities, people lit bonfires on hills, at crossroads, and at the edges of forests. These were special places. Fire was believed to have cleansing properties, including protecting against

evil forces. To make this defense more effective, herbs were thrown into the fire, such as mugwort, which people also used to fumigate their homes. Young women would gather around the fire, dancing in a circle and singing. Young men would show off their agility by jumping through the flames. Then, holding hands, the young people would jump in pairs, and a successful jump would cement the affection between them and herald marriage. Cattle were also driven through the fires to protect the livestock from disease.

Unmarried women would make wreaths of flowers and herbs and float them on local waterways to discover their fortunes. If someone's wreath flowed quickly, it meant that they would soon find love. If it got stuck in the reeds, it was a bad omen. Bachelors, meanwhile, would try to fish out the wreaths from the water. The more they found, and the faster they did it, the better.

Have you heard of the mysterious fern flower? According to folktales, it bloomed for a very short time on a single night, somewhere in the depths of the forest. Only a kind and noble person could find it. The search was dangerous because the flower was protected by treacherous forces. But it was worth the risk because it brought wealth, happiness, and prosperity to the person who found it. Whether or not people really believed in the existence of the mythical flower, they were eager to search for it.

The Kupala Night celebrations also involved immersion in water. Some people think it was this custom that gave the holiday its name, as *kupatsia* means "to bathe" in East Slavic languages. Others believe that the name related to jumping "toward the fire": *ku pału*. Still others think it referred to the name of a Slavic goddess. But leaving these disputes aside, the important thing was that people should not approach any bodies of water before that night. According to folk beliefs, unfriendly water spirits were rife at that time. After the holiday, bathing became safe again.

The rituals associated with Kupala Night became deeply rooted and continued even when Slavic beliefs were replaced by Christianity. Representatives of the church tried to discourage the population from following the old customs, but in the end it was easier to try to link them with Christian rituals. So Kupala Night was combined with the eve of the feast day of Saint John, which fell on the night of June 23. This change in the date of Kupala Night was the origin of Saint John's Eve—an equally extraordinary and enchanting celebration, except that it was under the patronage of John the Baptist, but still connected with water, since in Christian teachings Saint John baptized Jesus in the Jordan River.

Nowadays, on Kupala Night, or Saint John's Eve, the rituals are mainly for fun, although for certain pagan groups it is still an important holiday. Concerts are organized. People still make or buy wreaths and float them on the water, but the emphasis is more on the beauty of the flower arrangements than the prediction of weddings. And people still gather around fires. Interestingly, in some villages, the custom of burning tires on Saint John's Eve has endured. This probably relates to the old tradition of placing a wooden cart wheel in the Kupala Night bonfire, its shape being associated with the sun. When carts were no longer in use, tires became the equivalent.

In Sweden, celebrations at this time of year are very similar to Kupala Night. There, Midsummer is a nonworking holiday. It is celebrated on the last Friday before Saint John's Eve. People wear wreaths, sing joyful songs, and dance around a pole decorated with flowers. There is also a tradition of marriage fortune-telling. People collect seven or nine different types of flowers and hide them under their pillow. The idea is that they will dream of their future spouse. The holiday is also an opportunity to eat together, and the typical festive table includes potatoes and herring.

Mid-Autumn Festival

On this night, the full moon is said to appear especially large and bright. And indeed, at this point in its orbit, the moon is very close to Earth. It is a great time to admire the night sky while eating mooncakes. You can search the moon's surface for the Jade Rabbit, who helps Chang'e grind medicines and prepare the elixir of immortality in the Moon Palace, also called *Guǎnghán Gōng* (the Palace of Vast and Cold).

This Chinese holiday falls on the fifteenth day of the eighth lunar month (in the Gregorian calendar, this is the end of September or beginning of October). The traditions associated with Mid-Autumn Festival are said to be three thousand years old. The holiday is celebrated under other names and with local variations, including in Japan and Vietnam. Initially, it was a festival held at the end of the harvest period, but over time the significance of this aspect faded. Chinese writers and poets were full of praise for the full moon. Because its round shape symbolizes reconciliation and completeness, the evening of this holiday should be spent with loved ones. If this is not possible,

people will look at the sky, comforted by the knowledge that distant friends and family are looking at the same moon and sending warm thoughts.

In the evening, people go out to admire exhibitions of lanterns of various colors and shapes in the streets and parks. Lit lanterns are also released into the sky. Getting together to share a big meal and make wishes is an essential part of the celebrations. The special delicacies served include round fruits and, most importantly, mooncakes. Can you guess their shape? That's right—the same as the full moon! The mooncakes are thick, heavy with filling, and decorated on top with a distinctive pattern. The dough itself is sweet, made of flour, oil, and honey or syrup, but the fillings can be sweet or savory. They depend on the region and range from red bean paste, fruits, and nut and seed mixtures to ham and salted duck-egg yolk. It is common practice to exchange mooncakes with other people. The more important a person is to you, the more special the gift you want to give them, so mooncakes can be

purchased in very sophisticated and expensive packaging. These delicacies are given to people you respect, such as family members and friends.

And what is the background to this custom? There is a beautiful legend which, as often happens with legends, has many versions. According to one account, in ancient times ten suns unexpectedly rose above Earth. People suffered from the heat and there was a terrible drought. The brave archer Hou Yi managed to shoot down the nine excess suns, and in return, the gods gave him the elixir of immortality. But there was only enough for one person. Hou Yi loved his wife Chang'e very much and didn't want to see her grow old and die. He told her to hide the elixir. But Hou Yi's wicked apprentice learned about the elixir's power. While Hou Yi was away, his apprentice tried to take the elixir by force. Chang'e preferred to drink it herself rather than give it to someone like him. When she did, she gained immortality, but she could not remain on Earth. On the fifteenth day of the eighth month, she ascended to the moon, where she lived in the Moon Palace. Her husband looked at the moon's surface and felt such longing that he prepared some cakes to symbolically offer to his wife.

The presence of the rabbit at Chang'e's side is explained by another story taken from the Buddhist Jātaka tales. One day, a hungry old man asked some animals to share some food with him. The monkey brought fruit and the fox brought something it had hunted, but the rabbit, because it ate grass, had nothing the man could eat. So the rabbit decided to offer itself and threw itself into the fire. It turned out that the old man was a holy sage, or (in some versions) the Lord of Heaven himself. Impressed by the rabbit's willingness to sacrifice itself, he saved it from the flames and carried it to the moon so that everyone could admire it there. On the moon, the rabbit made friends with Chang'e.

In Japan, this amiable animal is thought to be grinding neither medicines nor the elixir of immortality, but ingredients for delicious mochi rice cakes. And the oldest legends placed another animal on the moon—a toad!

The legend is well commemorated in China, having inspired the names of the Chinese space mission Chang'e and the lunar rover Yutu—the Jade Rabbit.

Yaldā Night

The night of the winter solstice (usually December 21 in the northern hemisphere) is the longest night of the year. It is a time of darkness, heralding the arrival of winter. Iranians usually spend this darkest night, called Shab-e Chelleh or Yaldā Night, with their loved ones, entertaining each other with stories. After this night, things get easier, as the light starts to increase day by day.

Like Nowruz, this family holiday is celebrated not only in Iran but also in other countries of the former Persian Empire. It dates back to ancient rituals in honor of the solar deity Mithra, in whose form light was supposed to be reborn after the solstice. The holiday was later assimilated into Zoroastrianism, and on the longest night the god Ahura Mazda was believed to triumph over darkness and evil. Since it was an ominous time, people tried to protect themselves with various rituals; it was important to stay vigilant and to tend fires carefully.

Nowadays, the holiday is no longer religious. Families and friends meet, usually in the home of an elder, around the table. Often, the table is a *korsi*, a traditional Iranian piece of furniture used in winter that is low and square with a heater underneath it, and people sit on pillows or blankets laid out on the floor. A pot filled with coals is placed under the table, which is covered with a tablecloth, so the warmth flows from

the shared table quite literally. Red fruits are served as snacks, because their color is associated with the rising sun, and people also like to wear red on this night. Common fruits are pomegranates, watermelons (which are also supposed to ensure health during the winter months), black grapes, persimmons, and apples. Dried and candied fruits, pistachios, and other nuts are also eaten. Main dishes depend on the region: in Shiraz, for example, a dish called *kalam polo* is prepared from rice with aromatic herbs, kohlrabi, meatballs, and pomegranate paste. However, it is the snacks that are most important.

Guests sit up late into the night listening to music and sharing stories, fables, and anecdotes. They also tell fortunes based on the poems of Hafez. It is said that Hafez has the answer to all questions. On Yaldā Night, people open a collection of his works at random and read specific verses, then look for an interpretation.

Christmas

The best known of the Christian holidays, Christmas prompts people to come together and act with kindness. It brings to mind sparkling snow, a fire roaring in the fireplace, a beautifully decorated tree with a pile of gifts underneath, and Santa Claus—an old man with a long beard, dressed in red trousers, coat, and hat, racing across the sky in a sleigh to deliver presents. But this picture might be misleading, because Christmas doesn't look the same everywhere.

This holiday is also celebrated in places where there is no snow, and instead of fir trees, people decorate banana leaves or mango trees (in India, for example). In New Zealand, the standard Christmas tree is a local species of a deciduous tree, the expansive *pōhutukawa*, which blossoms with red flowers so doesn't need additional decorations.

And Santa Claus wasn't always pictured the way he is today. The popular image of the kindhearted, chubby grandfather figure was popularized by an American ad for Coca-Cola in 1931. Prior to that, his image was modeled on the Christian bishop Saint Nicholas of Myra, so he wore a bishop's robe and a pointed cap, and carried a long staff with a spiral handle, called a crosier. Even the red coat is not consistent: the Korean Santa Claus, called Santa Haraboji (meaning "Grandfather Santa"), is most often dressed in blue or green.

In some places, Santa is helped by elves in green jackets (in the United States), and in others by his granddaughter, the Snow Maiden (in Russia, where Santa is called Ded Moroz, or "Grandfather Frost"). Sometimes gifts are brought by elves (in Norway), Saint Basil (in Greece), or the baby Jesus (in Southwest Poland, Austria, and Germany), and they might be found not under the tree but in a stocking or sock. The gifts are also given at different times: sometimes on the evening of December 24, after Christmas Eve dinner, sometimes on the morning of December 25, and sometimes even in January.

In many parts of the world, Christmas is celebrated on December 25, although in the Orthodox Church it falls about two weeks later, because—as you might remember—in that tradition, holidays are marked according to the Julian calendar. In many languages, the name of the holiday suggests the reason for the celebration: it marks the birthday of Jesus Christ, believed by Christians to be the son of God, who came into the world as the child of Mary and Joseph. According to the biblical story, the couple had to travel to Bethlehem. When they couldn't find a place in any of the inns, they stopped for the night in a shepherd's cave—sometimes called a stable or a manger—and Jesus was born there. In Mexico, this search for a room is acted out in processions that take place during the pre-Christmas festival. According to the traditional story, Jesus's birth was accompanied by an extraordinary phenomenon in the sky, when the star of Bethlehem shone upon him.

In the early days of Christianity, Christmas wasn't celebrated at all. It began about three centuries after Jesus was born. The date was set symbolically because no one knew exactly when the birth took place. So why was this particular time chosen? Well, it was tied to the December winter solstice, which has a special significance in many pre-Christian traditions. During this period, rituals were dedicated to the shortest day of the year, and deities associated with the sun and crops were celebrated. So the church authorities were able to link the holiday with earlier, strongly rooted customs, and thus convince people to accept the new religion.

We have already learned that in ancient Persia people celebrated the birth of Mithra, the god of the sun and light. In Ancient Rome, celebrations were held in honor of Sol Invictus, the "Unconquered Sun." In the second half of December, the Romans celebrated the joyful Saturnalia, and it was probably there that the custom of family visits, exchanging gifts, and celebratory meals originated. Interestingly, in honor of Saturn, the Romans decorated evergreen trees. However, the Christian tradition of decorating a Christmas tree came later, only five hundred years ago, in Alsace, on the border of Germany and France, from where it gradually spread. At first, decorating was popular only among the upper classes, but nowadays Christmas decorations are found almost everywhere the holiday is celebrated.

Christmas traditions in the United States come from all over the world. Some families begin their celebrations with a dinner on Christmas Eve, similar to Poland and Germany. Others have a big meal on Christmas Day, like in the United Kingdom. Many children want to make sure Santa and his reindeer are well fed for their long night of delivering presents, so they leave out milk and cookies for Santa, and carrots for the reindeer. Counting down the days until Christmas is also important, with many children using Advent calendars that begin on December 1. Each day leading up to Christmas features a "door" that reveals something like a small gift or decoration.

In Poland, the celebrations begin on the evening of December 24, with a dinner called Wigilia. The dinner is also sometimes named Gwiazdka, or "Little Star," after the custom—also known in Ukraine—that you can sit down at the table when the first star is visible in the sky. Often, all members of the household are involved in preparing the

dinner, which consists of traditional meat-free dishes, such as beet soup, dumplings with poppy seeds, and cabbage with mushrooms. There should be twelve dishes, one for each month of the year (or, as some say, the number of Jesus's disciples). Ortho-dox Christians also celebrate with a meat-free dinner consisting of twelve dishes and a beautifully decorated Christmas tree, and share prosphora, or blessed bread.

In other countries, meat-free dishes are not always part of the tradition: for example, in Germany, meat is commonly served at Christmas Eve dinner. In Poland and Lithuania, it is customary to share a thin, crisp wafer with loved ones before the meal, and an additional place is usually set at the table for an unexpected guest.

Christmas Eve was once considered a magical time when unusual things could happen—for example, it was believed that domestic and farm animals could speak with human voices. After Christmas Eve dinner, those who are religious participate in a special church service, the midnight mass. In the Philippines, the mass is held at 10 p.m., and only after that do families sit down for dinner, which can last until dawn. Filipinos often light fireworks at Christmas too. Copts (Egyptian Christians) also sit down to eat after a 10 p.m. mass, which lasts about four hours, or even until dawn in some cathedrals. Copts celebrate according to the Julian calendar, but they sometimes decorate Christmas trees (usually artificial, as real ones can only be imported at great expense) in time for the Gregorian calendar's Christmas Eve.

Koreans celebrate Christmas Eve very casually, by going to a restaurant or a kara-oke bar.

In Australia, December falls in the middle of summer. Temperatures reaching over 80 degrees Fahrenheit (around 30 degrees Celsius) are not conducive to preparing a big feast, so Christmas is usually a time to relax for many, either on the beach or at a barbecue with friends and family. Many Australians enjoy singing carols. Carols by Candlelight is a custom dating back to the 1930s, involving meeting after sunset for carol concerts in the open air. The audience brings candles and sings along with the performers.

In Ethiopia, Christmas is celebrated according to the Julian calendar. Processions go from church to church all night long. During the mass, the priest and the congregation sing, dance, and play musical instruments. On Christmas Day, people go to church wearing a *shamma*, a shawl made of white fabric with patterned edges that is wrapped around the body. There is a game that is usually played at Christmas called *genna*, which is similar to field hockey. According to legend, the shepherds invented *genna* on the night of Jesus's birth. Genna is also the Ethiopian name for the entire holiday, so if you want to say "Merry Christmas" in Ethiopia's national language, Amharic, you say, "Melkam Genna."

In Finland and Estonia, visiting saunas is popular at Christmas.

People in Greece and Cyprus have some interesting Christmas superstitions. To bribe the *kallikantzaroi*, mischievous creatures that roam the earth between December 24 and January 6, people leave treats for them on their roofs. They also use other methods to prevent the pranksters from entering their homes.

In Germany and Austria, children who have misbehaved have to watch out for Krampus, a creature resembling a devil with hooves and horns, who uses a pitchfork to pack little rascals into his big basket.

Children in Iceland also have to be on their guard. There, a huge cat called Jólakötturinn prowls around and devours those who have not received new clothes, which means they haven't fulfilled their household duties. A little scarier than the threat of Santa bringing a piece of coal!

Hanukkah

Candle flames twinkle cheerfully, potato pancakes sizzle in oil, beautiful songs resound around the house, and dreidels spin on the table. This is Hanukkah, also called Chag HaUrim, the Festival of Lights.

According to the Hebrew calendar, Hanukkah begins on the twenty-fifth day of the month of Kislev and ends on the second day of Tevet (in the Gregorian calendar, both dates are usually in December). It commemorates the story of a miracle that happened in ancient Judea. In the second century BCE, this region was ruled by the Syrian-Hellenistic Seleucid dynasty, which tried to impose Greek religion and culture on the local population. Many Jews were not happy about this. They faced cruel persecution because of their faith. It finally became too much when King Antiochus IV Epiphanes desecrated the temple in Jerusalem, transforming it into a place of worship for the Greek god Zeus. An armed uprising broke out, and the Jewish rebels managed to defeat Antiochus's well-trained and much larger army. The temple was

recaptured. However, the statues of foreign gods had to be removed. Above all, the stolen menorah had to be replaced. The menorah is a seven- or nine-branched decorative candelabra, which symbolizes the presence of God when lit.

In those days, candles were not placed in the menorah like today. Instead, small oil lamps were used. Consecrated oil was used to light the menorah. Only a small jug of this oil was found in the recaptured temple, enough for just one day. But a miracle happened: the small quantity of oil lasted for the whole eight days needed to prepare new oil. On the twenty-fifth of Kislev, 165 BCE, the atmosphere was solemn as the temple was reconsecrated. In Hebrew, the word *hanukkah* means "inauguration, dedication."

The joyful celebration lasted eight days, the same length as the holiday period that commemorates it. The most important custom now is lighting candles for eight consecutive evenings in a special menorah called a *hanukkiah*. Each day of the holiday, a new candle is added—one on the first day, two on the second, three on the third, and so on, up to eight. According to tradition, it is forbidden to use the candles to light each other. There is a completely separate candle for this purpose, called the *shamash*, which means "helper" in Hebrew. The menorah has nine branches, to accommodate the eight main candles and the *shamash*. It is placed either at the entrance to the home or by a window, so that the light shines out, announcing the miracle of Hanukkah.

The holiday is a joyful time to spend with family. Household members gather around the *hanukkiah*, and the lighting of the candles (at sunset or at the sight of the first stars) is accompanied by songs and blessings. People eat nuts, candy, and—in memory of the extraordinary little oil jug from centuries ago—foods fried in oil, such as doughnuts, crêpes, and potato pancakes. Children receive little gifts, candy, or small amounts of money on the first night, the last night, or sometimes every night of the holiday.

Another Hanukkah tradition is playing dreidel, named for the spinning top used in the game. The dreidel has a Hebrew letter on each of its four sides: *nun*, *gimmel*, *hay*, and *shin*. Each letter is the beginning of a word, and these words form a sentence: *nes gadol haya sham*, which means

"a great miracle happened there." However in Israel, *pay* is used instead of *shin* for the sentence *nes gadol haya po*, meaning "a great miracle happened here." Which letter the dreidel falls on tells you what action to take in the game: *nun*, you don't give or take any game pieces; *gimmel*, you take everything; *hay*, you take half the pot; *shin* (or *pay*), you add one piece to the pot. The game pieces can be anything, but many families play with candy or chocolate coins. What a delicious game!

Saint Jordan's Day

Outside, the snow is sparkling. It creaks loudly underfoot. Despite the winter cold, people of all ages, including older people and parents with small children, walk in a solemn procession from the church to an ice-covered lake. At the head of the procession is a priest dressed in fine robes. The entourage carries icons, ceremonial banners, and processional crosses. There will be a blessing on the shore. This is the culmination of the festival of Saint Jordan's Day, celebrated in the Orthodox Church.

This holiday, also known as Epiphany, which falls on January 19 in the Julian calendar (January 6 in the Gregorian calendar), commemorates an important moment for Christians: the baptism of Jesus in the Jordan River. Baptism is a ceremony of admission into the Christian community. In most branches of Christianity, this event is only mentioned during the liturgy, but there are no special customs associated with it. But in the Orthodox Church, it is given great importance because it marks the founding of the community of believers.

On the day of the holiday, a service is held in the church. Then the congregation walks in procession to the water (a river, lake, or pond) where the consecration will take place. If there are no natural bodies of water nearby, a well near the church may be used instead. Symbolically, the river or lake becomes the Jordan River, and the worshippers relive the baptism of Jesus. Prayers and beautiful ceremonial singing take place on the shore. Every now and then, someone will call out, *Hospodi, pomiłuj*, meaning "Lord, have mercy." Orthodox liturgy is usually conducted in a language oth-

er than the national language, such as Church Slavonic. During the ceremony, the priest says a prayer to the Holy Spirit and immerses the cross in the water three times. Sometimes, white doves are released into the sky, symbolizing the Holy Spirit. A three-branched candelabra (representing the Trinity of Father, Son, and Holy Spirit) is also immersed. Finally, blessed water is sprinkled on the congregation. Some people also wash their faces or hands in the lake or river. The congregation also fills vessels with the blessed water to take home. In ancient times, apart from religious purposes, this water was used for various medicinal treatments.

On the eve of Saint Jordan's Day, a strict fast is observed. The first blessing of the water takes place in the church, as a reminder of the baptism of all believers. Prepa-

rations are also made for the later stage of the celebrations. A cross and a makeshift altar are set up on the bank or shore where the second, main blessing of the water will take place. If the lake or pond is covered with ice, a hole must be made in the shape of a cross. Families sit down to share a meat-free dinner. In the past, people would wander from house to house, a bit like carolers, offering New Year wishes in the form of poems.

Saint Jordan's Day is celebrated in many countries, including Ukraine, Russia, Belarus, Lithuania, and Poland.

Diwali

The Indian festival of Diwali (also known as Deepavali) is also called the Festival of Lights. It is accompanied by the glow of the flames of dozens of clay oil lamps, *rangoli* decorations, and joyful commotion. It symbolizes the victory of light over darkness, of good over evil, and people like to celebrate such an important occasion with a bang. Fireworks and firecrackers explode, making so much noise in the largest cities that it's almost impossible to sleep, and crowds party together in the streets.

This Hindu festival is usually dedicated to Lakshmi, the goddess of abundance and fertility. It is celebrated all over India, but the associated customs and beliefs differ depending on the region. In the north, for example, it signifies the start of a new year, and is intended to commemorate the events described in the epic *Ramayana*—specifically, the victory of the titular hero Rama over his nemesis Ravana, who abducted his wife, Sita.

Usually, all the festivities that make up Diwali last for five days, and the main celebrations take place during the new moon, when fireworks are launched into the sky.

In the Gregorian calendar, Diwali falls between mid-October and mid-November; in the Hindu calendar, at the end of the month Ashwin and the beginning of Kartika. In preparation for the holiday, people clean their homes thoroughly and also shop for new clothes, candy, and decorations. The holiday is a time for family visits, small gifts, and shared meals.

Diwali marks the end of the summer harvest and the beginning of winter. It coincides with the new moon, which is considered the darkest night of the Hindu calendar—hence the need to brighten it up. Traditional lamps called *diyas* have an elongated, teardrop shape. They are made of clay and filled with melted clarified butter or vegetable oil, such as linseed, in which the wick is immersed. Nowadays, people also use ready-made decorative lanterns, which don't need to be filled with oil.

The *rangoli* decorations used during Diwali are intricate geometric designs made from colorful powders, embellished with *diyas* and flowers or petals. Whole families and neighborhoods get involved in the preparations. *Rangoli* is placed on the floors of houses, temples, restaurants, and shops. As with many other Indian holidays, floral garlands are also ubiquitous, and religious people go to temples during this time.

As for the custom of fireworks, the emphasis now is placed instead on a quiet Diwali celebrated by candlelight, among beautiful decorations, with family.

Diwali is celebrated not only by Hindus but also by Sikhs (whose most important spiritual site, the Golden Temple in Amritsar, shines with thousands of lights), Jains, and some Indian Buddhists.

Ramadan and Eid al-Fitr

When a thin crescent moon shines in the night sky heralding the beginning of the month of Shawwal, Muslims around the world begin celebrations for Eid al-Fitr, a joyful holiday that ends Ramadan, a period of fasting and sacrifice. There is an atmosphere of laughter and warmth, and people wish each other *Eid mubarak*, or "blessed feast/festival."

Fasting is one of the five pillars of Islam, and therefore a duty for Muslims (the other pillars are hajj (pilgrimage to Mecca), prayer, charity, and profession of faith). The period of fasting takes place in the ninth month of the Islamic lunar calendar, which is called Ramadan. Just like the other months, it lasts twenty-nine or thirty days. The length of the months in the Islamic calendar is changeable: if the moon can be seen on the twenty-ninth night of the month, the next month begins, but when the moon is not visible, the month will last thirty days. That means that the exact start date of Ramadan is flexible, depending on the geographical location and weather conditions. And because the Islamic year is shorter than a solar year, Ramadan (like the other months of the Islamic calendar) shifts by ten or eleven days every year, migrating through different periods of the Gregorian calendar and falling some years when the days are short and some when they are long. Why does this matter? Because during the period of fasting, people can't eat or drink anything for the entire day, from dawn until sunset. This is a huge sacrifice, especially in the summertime in countries where it is very hot.

Ramadan, also called the holy month, is a time of penance, prayer, working on one's character, helping others, making amends for one's sins, and turning toward God, called Allah in Islam. Followers of Islam believe that it was during Ramadan that the archangel Jibril (known as Gabriel in the Christian tradition) revealed the first verses of the Quran, the holy book of Islam, to Muhammad. Jibril also appointed Muhammad a prophet: a person who conveys God's will to the people.

The period of fasting is also intended to make people sensitive to the lives of those who are poor and hungry, giving an insight into their everyday experience. People are reminded to do good deeds and focus on *zakat* (or charity), another pillar of Islam.

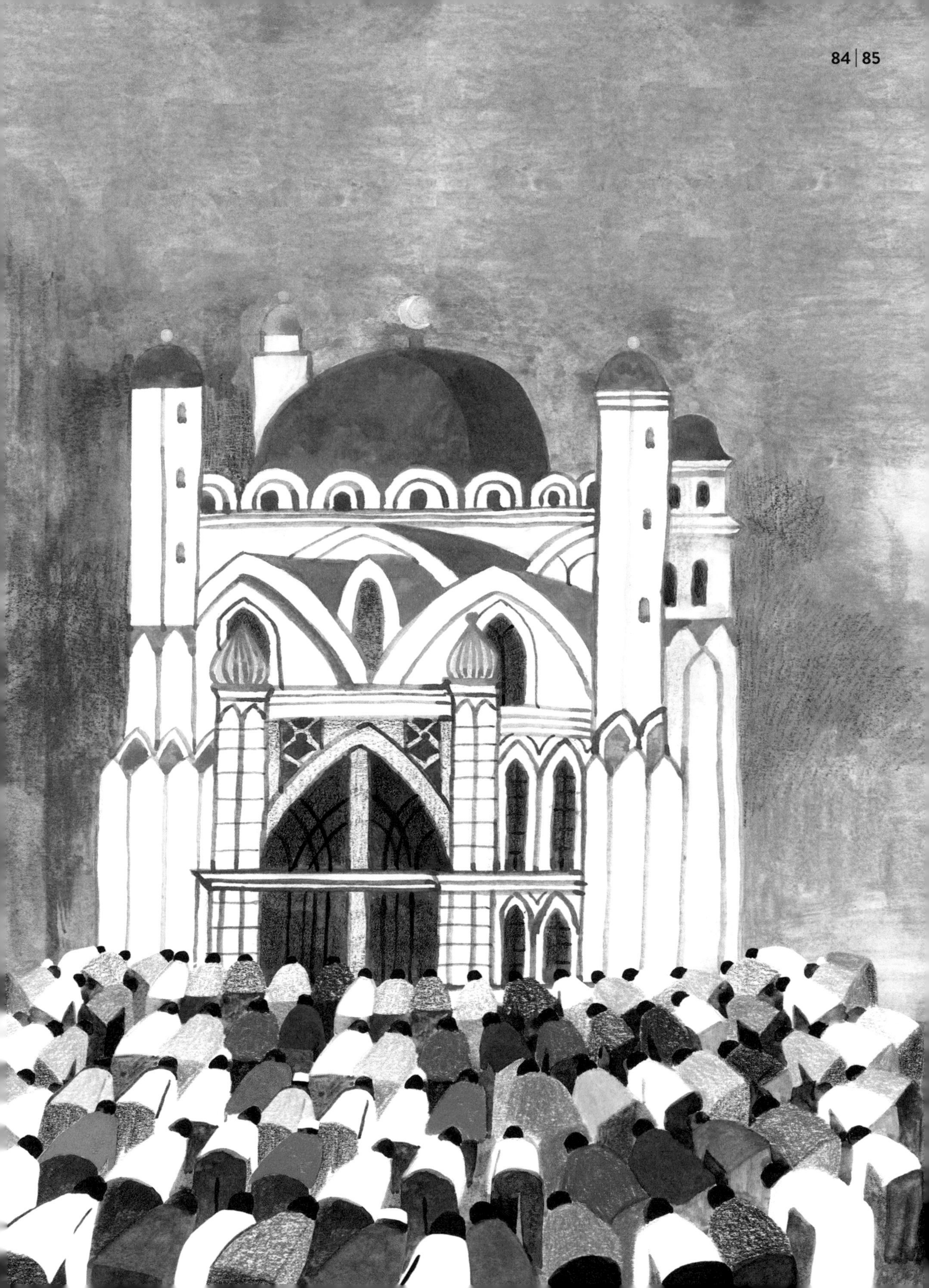

Fasting during Ramadan is obligatory for all adults, with the exception of those who are sick, pregnant or breastfeeding, or traveling. However, these groups are encouraged to make up for it by fasting at a later date. Children don't have to fast, but as they get older, they gradually start to do so on some days during the month.

Two meals are eaten each day during Ramadan: one before sunrise and the other after sunset. The first is called *suhur*. It is served before sunrise, so in summer it can be very early, and people might go back to sleep after eating. The second meal is called *iftar*. This dinner can turn into a lavish feast. People invite each other to their homes or meet in restaurants. As a result, in countries that are majority Muslim, there is more traffic in the evenings since everyone is in a hurry to join their loved ones. After sunset, the fast should be broken as soon as possible, which is traditionally done by drinking water and eating three dates, just as the prophet Muhammad did when he broke his own fast. Sweet dishes are an important part of the *iftar* table, with so many sugary treats consumed that the holiday is sometimes called "Sweet Eid." One of the popular Ramadan delicacies is *knafeh*: a cookie stuffed with cheese and nuts, covered with sweet syrup, and sprinkled with crushed pistachios. The whole community might be invited to participate in this feast, and friends or neighbors of different faiths will sit together to share a meal.

In Muslim countries, life has a different rhythm during Ramadan. Hotels serve *suhur* buffets in the early morning hours, when the kitchen would normally be closed. Most restaurants are closed during the day. Adults may work shorter hours and children leave school earlier than usual. Offices and institutions close around noon, then open again in the evening and operate until late at night. Special cooking shows are broadcast on TV, giving advice on nutritious morning meals to help people get through a day of fasting. Seasonal wishes are woven into the ads. Homes, shop windows, and public spaces are decorated with lights, stars, crescents (often embellished with beautiful ornaments), and *fanous* lanterns, a tradition that began in Egypt and has spread across the Muslim world.

Eid al-Fitr is the end of the fasting period. It is not only a celebration that fasting is over but also a time to give thanks to Allah for the strength that was necessary to persevere through all the sacrifice. The festival lasts for two or three days and is an opportunity to meet with friends and

relatives, to exchange small gifts, and to finally feast unreservedly. Eid al-Fitr should be honored in appropriate style, by either wearing one's best clothes or buying completely new ones. First, though, people pray together in the mosque and make donations as a sign of solidarity, so that people in difficult circumstances can also afford to celebrate. It is a time of reconciliation and unity.

The word *eid* itself means "festival" or "feast." Eid al-Fitr is sometimes called the "Lesser Eid" to distinguish it from the second Eid, Eid al-Adha, the Feast of Sacrifice.

Vesak

According to legend, over two and a half thousand years ago Queen Mayadevi was journeying through the mountainous regions of what is now Nepal to visit her family. She was pregnant. The baby didn't wait until they reached their destination; he was born during the journey. No one knew that centuries later, this event would be a reason for joy and celebration for so many people.

The boy was named Siddhartha and his family name was Gautama. The birth was accompanied by unusual omens, and the sage Asita predicted that a special future lay in wait for the child. The prince grew up surrounded by wealth and luxury, but when he reached adulthood, he left his home to learn about the lives and struggles of ordinary people. He became an enlightened sage and preacher, known as the Buddha, and developed the basic principles of Buddhism. The word *buddha* means "enlightened one" in Sanskrit.

On the full moon (first or second, depending on the country) of the fourth month of the Buddhist lunar calendar, Buddhists all over the world celebrate the Buddha's birthday, and sometimes—depending on the branch of Buddhism—also his enlightenment and death. According to the Gregorian calendar, this date falls in April or May. The holiday has different names depending on the place. Vesak is one of the most common.

A primary belief of Buddhism is not to harm other beings and to help others, which is why good deeds should be performed on this day. People donate blood, give money, and visit older people. Sometimes in majority Buddhist countries the state authorities also perform acts of kindness. In Sri Lanka, for example, the president grants amnesty to several hundred prisoners on this day. Beautiful light displays are arranged. People visit temples from dawn until dusk, offering gifts to the monks, burning incense and candles, and laying flowers. Visitors to the temples are also served food. People pour water on statues of the Buddha to wash away their own bad deeds, and birds are released into the sky. It is customary to walk around the temple three times holding a candle, in memory of the three "jewels" of Buddhism: the Buddha, the Dharma (Buddha's teachings), and the Sangha (the monastic community).

In Indonesia and Mongolia on this day, dozens of lanterns are released into the sky. In Malaysia, there are joyful processions in the streets. People dress in white or yellow and carry pink candles in the shape of lotus flowers—the lotus is a symbol of enlightenment, purity, and rebirth. The processions also feature floats with images of the Buddha, decorated with lights and flowers, prepared by temples and various organizations. Chanting flows from loudspeakers, and monks bless passers-by.

Above all, Vesak—which is designated an international holiday by UNESCO—is a time of joy and prayers for peace around the world.

Durga Puja

The key figure during this multiday festival is the Hindu goddess Durga—a fearless and invincible warrior riding a lion or tiger. She has many arms, with each hand holding a symbol or weapon, such as a bow and arrows, a sword, and a trident. She might look scary, but there's no need to fear . . . unless you're a demon. It was Durga who saved the people and the gods from the frightful Mahishasura. The holiday Durga Puja—a *puja* (ritual in honor of a deity) dedicated to Durga—is celebrated in memory of this victory.

According to the traditional story, the buffalo-demon Mahishasura received a useful reward from the gods for his services. They promised him that he would be virtually invincible and that only a woman would be able to defeat him. Mahishasura became very bold. The demons in his service roamed the earth, and Mahishasura himself challenged the gods—who, due to their rash gift, couldn't defeat him. However, their anger led to the birth of the goddess Durga. Mahishasura approached her with disdain. She was unaccompanied, and he thought that she was too delicate and pretty to fight. He even proposed to her. But Durga rejected his advances, announcing that she would only marry the one who defeated her in battle. Despite cunningly changing form several times, Mahishasura lost the battle, and the triumphant goddess beheaded him.

Durga Puja is celebrated in the month of Ashwin in the Hindu calendar (mid-September to mid-October in the Gregorian calendar), primarily in the eastern and northeastern parts of India, especially West Bengal, and in neighboring Bangladesh. Durga's victory over Mahishasura is also celebrated in other regions of India, with slight variations in the customs, and under different names. Durga Puja lasts over a week, with the last few days of the celebration being the most important, and there are different rituals for each day. People pray and make offerings of sweets, rice, and flowers to the goddess.

The holiday is celebrated most magnificently in the city of Kolkata, which comes alive with an unusual rhythm during this time. Public transport runs more frequently, many shops are closed, and popular restaurants are fully booked. Whole families

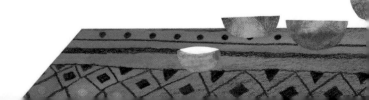

visit *pandals*, special temporary structures, until late at night. These structures are beautifully decorated and contain images and statues of Durga defeating Mahisha-sura. Durga is often accompanied by four other deities, said to be her children: the elephant-headed Ganesha, the goddesses Lakshmi and Saraswati, and the warrior Kartikeya. Every year the *pandals* look different, and their creators try to outdo each other in inventiveness.

Local communities organize the construction of the *pandals*. They either build them themselves or hire specialists. Committees are set up to collect funds for the build. There's even a competition for the most beautiful *pandal*.

It is believed that Durga visits her devotees during Durga Puja. At the beginning of the celebrations, the goddess must be awakened by a priest. Durga becomes present in anything made in her image after a ritual known as "offering the eyes," in which the eyes are painted on idols of the goddess. The idol statues are made of natural materials, such as clay, straw, and bamboo. One of the districts in Kolkata is home to

a number of sculptors who prepare images of deities for this and other holidays. The clay for these figures comes from the nearby Hooghly River.

On the third day of the celebration, a female child is selected to be worshipped as a goddess. The girl must fast all day long, as a sign of purification and dedication, and people scatter offerings of flowers around her.

The Hooghly River, along with other bodies of water, plays an important role in the festival. On the last day of Durga Puja, the goddess's victory over the demon is celebrated, and Durga's presence leaves the statues and returns home. The idols, now "empty," have to be returned to nature. They are brought out from the *pandals* and

taken to the river, where they are immersed in the water. Trucks rumble through the city to the waterfront, transporting the statues as well as the singing, joyful people who are taking part in the ceremony. Since many of the statues are made of clay and straw, they do not harm the environment, and efforts are also made to use eco-friendly paints for their decoration.

On the last day of Durga Puja, it is customary for married women to smear their faces with vermilion, a bright red pigment, for good luck. Some women even wear this color along the parting in their hair. Red is also the dominant color of clothing at the end of Durga Puja. Then people have to wait another year until the goddess visits her followers again.

Eid al-Adha

The Feast of Sacrifice, Eid al-Adha, is the most important point in the religious calendar for Muslims, alongside Eid al-Fitr. The main idea of the holiday is entrusting oneself to Allah and trusting in his mercy.

It begins on the tenth day of the twelfth month of the Islamic calendar, Dhu al-Hijja, which is traditionally the time of the hajj, the pilgrimage to Mecca. Hajj is one of the five pillars of Islam, which means every devout Muslim who is able to must visit this Saudi city—home to the Kaaba, the holiest place in Islam—at least once in their life.

Although Eid al-Adha is associated with the hajj, it is celebrated by all Muslims, not just those who are on pilgrimage. The holiday commemorates the test, described in the Quran, that Allah gave to Ibrahim when he commanded Ibrahim to sacrifice his firstborn son, Ishmael. Full of sorrow, Ibrahim agreed, and Allah—moved by Ibrahim's obedience and devotion—ordered the boy to be spared and a lamb to be killed instead (or a goat, according to some versions). A similar version of these events is found in the Bible, which is why this story is known to Jews, Christians, and Muslims alike.

In memory of this, Muslims sacrifice a hoofed animal, such as a sheep, ram, cow, or goat. In Mecca, due to the huge number of pilgrims, this task is often entrusted to butchers, for a fee. The meat is divided into three equal parts: one to be given to those in need, another to be given to relatives, and the third to be eaten during a shared feast. Due to the abundance of meat dishes on the table, a contrast to the sweet celebrations of Ramadan, this holiday is sometimes called "Salty Eid" (it is also known as "Big Eid").

Much like Eid al-Fitr, the Feast of Sacrifice is a time to wear new clothes, visit family and friends, give donations to charitable causes, and participate in prayers at the mosque. This is one of many occasions when women and girls decorate their hands with intricate patterns made of henna, a natural dye obtained from plants.

Easter

At Easter, the holiest day for Christians, great sadness meets great joy. Religious rituals intertwine with ancient folk customs, combining the biblical story of victory over death with the cycle of nature, which is awakening after its long winter sleep.

The beliefs related to Easter are the foundation of Christianity. This holiday commemorates the resurrection of Jesus, whom God sent to Earth to die for the people. Christians believe that this happened so that all sin could be forgiven, guaranteeing an eternal life after death and rebirth after Judgment Day. Jesus died as a martyr on the cross, a brutal form of execution used in the ancient world. He was considered a troublemaker because he preached about God and had gathered many followers. According to the biblical account, three days after his death a group of women visited the grave where his body was buried. There they found an angel who told them to spread the good news: Jesus had returned to life.

   The date of Easter changes each year—in the Gregorian calendar, it can fall anywhere between March 22 and April 25. How is the date determined? Easter is celebrated on the first Sunday after the first spring full moon. This is close to the date of the Jewish holiday of Passover, because according to the Bible, Jesus was crucified

on that day. The Orthodox Church sets its date according to the Julian calendar, so in Orthodox churches Easter is celebrated thirteen days later than in other Christian denominations. Copts (Egyptian Christians) also celebrate Easter on this later date.

Easter is celebrated by all Christians, but different customs are observed depending on the country and the denomination. The holiday is preceded by forty days of Lent, when believers, commemorating Jesus's forty-day fast, should refrain from partying and eating rich or fatty foods, including meat. Some people give up their favorite pastimes during Lent. In ancient times, fasting was observed much more strictly, in part for practical reasons: it was a period when supplies were running low and there were still no new crops, so food had to be rationed.

The last week before Easter is called Holy Week. During this week, events related to Easter are commemorated, starting with Jesus's entry into Jerusalem, when his followers welcomed him by laying palm leaves and cloaks on the road. On Palm Sunday,

various parts of trees are brought to church to be blessed, such as palm leaves (in Argentina), olive branches (in Italy), and catkins (in Czechia and Slovakia).

In parts of Europe, Easter palm decorations are a big deal. In the past, they were made from aquatic plants—such as grasses and reeds—as these were the first plants to regenerate after winter. The willow was deemed to have protective and magical properties. To this day, Easter palms are made from dried flowers and catkins entwined with green boxwood twigs. The form of the decorations depends on the region. In some places, people make and display beautiful palm decorations, several feet high, made of colorful dried flowers and grasses. Competitions are organized for the most beautiful palm decoration.

There are many folk beliefs associated with catkins from a blessed palm decoration. For example, eating them was once thought to ensure health. The palm decoration itself was supposed to protect the house against lightning strikes, ensure good crops, and help when farm animals were sick.

Another important day in Holy Week is Maundy Thursday, when the last supper of Jesus and his disciples is remembered. This event is seen as the origin of the rite of the Christian mass or service, where believers come together in worship every Sunday.

Good Friday is commemorated as the day of Jesus's death. Night vigils are held at symbolic graves set up inside churches for the Easter period. In the Philippines, people take part in the famous Passion play, during which the events of Jesus's final hours are reenacted. Passion plays and processions are also popular in other countries with large Christian populations.

In the Orthodox Church, the Good Friday ceremonies and liturgy have a very solemn and mournful character.

Holy Saturday is a time of waiting. While other churches may choose to have services, it is the only day when no services are held in the Catholic Church. In some parts of Europe, Christians bring food to the church on Holy Saturday to be blessed. In Poland, the food is carried in a wicker basket decorated with boxwood, catkins, or spring flowers. Traditionally, the basket contains eggs (symbolizing new life), bread (representing the body of Jesus), sausage (signifying abundance), salt (for its cleansing properties), and a figure of a lamb made from butter or dough (symbolizing Jesus after his resurrection). The foods are eaten during breakfast on Easter Sunday; rather than serving to satisfy hunger, they have a ritual significance.

In Finland, children dress up as witches on Holy Saturday and go from house to house with decorated willow twigs to wish people good fortune in exchange for candy, a bit like Halloween.

On Easter Sunday, in all places where Easter is celebrated, a special mass is held at 6 a.m., and the church bells ring to announce the joyful news of the resurrection, since it is believed that Jesus rose from the grave during the night. Later in the day, families sit down for a meal at a table set with traditional dishes, which differ depending on the region.

In English-speaking countries, as well as in Germany and France, adults hide colorful eggs—especially chocolate ones—in homes and gardens for children to find. In many places, there is also a custom of receiving small gifts "from the Easter bunny." As an animal associated with fertility, the rabbit is one of the symbols of Easter, due to the new life of spring.

Easter celebrations in Mexico last fourteen days, with an extra week of observance after Easter Sunday, but Easter Sunday is celebrated with the most excitement. People dance and feast in the open air at big street parties, accompanied by fireworks.

In Poland and Slovakia, there is an enduring folk custom of people pouring water on each other on Easter Monday for fun and good luck. In rural areas, farmers "bless" their fields with an Easter palm decoration dipped in water.

In modern times, Easter is strongly associated with eggs, which symbolize rebirth and new life. Historically, before Christianity, they were very important in many traditions and cultures—the Slavs, for example, used eggs in various ceremonies related to the dead. The custom of bringing eggs to graves continued in Poland until the nineteenth century. Initially, church leaders forbade their inclusion in Easter rituals because they were associated with old customs. Eggs were used to break curses, ward off diseases, and cast love spells.

In many countries, eggs are dyed and decorated, and not just for Easter. As we already know, painted eggs are sometimes used to decorate the table during Nowruz. People in Southeast Asia were painting eggs as early as the third century BCE.

There are many legends to explain why eggs are dyed at Easter. One of the most beautiful comes from Greece: As Mary Magdalene, one of Jesus's followers, sat crying outside his empty tomb, an angel appeared. The angel announced the resurrection

and told Mary to spread the news. When Mary returned home, she discovered that all the eggs she kept in a bowl had turned red. As she was spreading the angel's news, she handed the eggs out to Jesus's apostles (twelve men who shared Jesus's teachings), and birds emerged from the shells and flew away.

In some countries, people play Easter games with hard-boiled eggs by banging then against one another. The winner is the person whose egg remains intact. As a prize, they get to eat the eggs used in the game.

Many people also decorate their houses for Easter, with many of the decorations associated with the coming of spring. In Poland, catkins and spring flowers (such as daffodils or tulips) are displayed, and decorations feature Easter eggs, chickens, lambs, and rabbits. In Germany, people hang colorful eggs on small trees, or on individual branches placed in vases. Scandinavians fill their houses with yellow flowers and branches of birch and willow.

Busójárás and Other Costume Carnivals

In the Christian tradition, Carnival is the period after Christmas and before the tranquil period of Lent. It is thought to originate from ancient Greek and Roman festivals, such as Saturnalia. This is an extraordinary and rebellious time. In many places it is still accompanied by colorful and lively rituals, as in the Hungarian town of Mohács, where people in wooden devil masks and animal skins parade in the streets for several days.

As we have learned, Lent traditionally means making sacrifices: giving up partying temporarily as well as modifying the diet, particularly refraining from eating meat. The word "carnival" is thought to be associated with this custom, coming from the Latin *carne vale*, meaning "meat, farewell." Before the fasting period, it was necessary to let off steam. Carnival was therefore a time of unrestrained fun, amusement, and the reversal of the usual order of things—when a jester could be king and the king could be a jester—and people could get away with doing what they couldn't usually

do, including pranks. Carnival traditions date back to the Middle Ages and include masquerades, street performances, dances, and processions. Nowadays, Carnival is mainly an opportunity to organize parties, but some interesting folk customs have also survived.

Busójárás, or the *busó* parade, takes place in the Hungarian town of Mohács, located close to the Croatian border. Some of the town's inhabitants are members of the Croatian ethnic minority Šokci. For six days, the town is taken over by the *busós*, who dress in wooden masks, baggy sheepskin coats, loose linen trousers, large leather boots, and cowbells. The masks are delightfully diverse, with no two designs the same.

The *busós* dance and frolic, behaving rudely, joking, and making noise with rattles and clappers. In the past, only young married men played the role of the masked creatures, but nowadays anyone can join in.

The origin of this custom dates back to the sixteenth century, when Hungary was occupied by the Ottoman Empire. Supposedly, the Šokci residents of Mohács, fearing the Turkish invaders, left their homes and hid in the nearby swamps. One stormy winter's night they were advised by a mysterious old man to return, dressed in scary

masks and sheepskins, while making a lot of noise. The terrified Turkish soldiers fled, convinced that a pack of demons was attacking them. Other versions of the legend emphasize chasing away not enemies but winter itself—and Busójárás includes a ritual to bid farewell to winter and welcome spring. For this purpose, winter's coffin is melted and a straw effigy that represents it is burned. Folklore performances are also held. In 2009, the *busó* festivities were included on UNESCO's Representative List of the Intangible Cultural Heritage of Humanity.

People who dress up in animal skins and wooden masks, carrying bells, can also be found in Sardinia, Croatia, Romania, Slovenia, and Bulgaria. As in Mohács, these festivities integrate local communities and attract curious tourists.

There are also parades of colorful costumes in the Polish tradition. Special Carnival customs are observed in Kuyavia in north-central Poland, where groups of people go from house to house in the period between Fat Thursday (the last Thursday before Lent) and Shrove Tuesday (the day before Lent starts), collecting donations of food and drink and wishing people good fortune.

They wear animal costumes with symbolic meanings: a bear for strength, a horse for vegetation, a stork to herald spring and abundance, and—particularly important in folk culture—a goat for fertility. The animals in the procession are sometimes accompanied by other characters, such as a bride and groom, the devil, or death.

At the end of Carnival, it is customary to indulge in various delicacies. In Poland, Fat Thursday is celebrated by eating doughnuts and sweet, deep-fried pastries called *faworki*. In the past, though, it wasn't sweets that reigned supreme on this day— in wealthy homes, people ate copious meat dishes, and poorer families feasted on cabbage and groats with crackling, sausages, and bacon. According to one folk saying, on Fat Thursday you should eat the same amount of fatty foods as the number of times the cat moves its tail!

Fat Thursday delicacies are also enjoyed in Germany. But in many places—including English-speaking countries, Sweden, and France—the day of gluttony falls on the final Tuesday before Lent, known as Shrove Tuesday. In the United States this day is commonly called Fat Tuesday, but in the United Kingdom it is called Pancake Day. Can you guess what people there eat on that day? In Sweden and Finland, the traditional sweet treat is *semla*—a cardamom-flavored wheat bun filled with almond paste and whipped cream.

The Orthodox pre-Lent celebration is called Maslenitsa, and its tradition dates back to ancient Slavic folk festivals for banishing winter and welcoming spring.

Carnival of Venice

If you visit Venice during Carnival, you might think that you've stumbled onto the set of a costume drama or been invited to a mysterious ball. There are processions of masked figures in strange regalia from bygone eras, torches light up the gondolas floating along the canals, and illuminations are projected on the buildings. For eleven days, life in the city changes completely as it is taken over by street magicians, fire eaters, musicians, and actors.

The Carnival of Venice always starts ten days before Ash Wednesday, the first day of Lent. The traditions of the celebration date back to the times when the city was its own republic. In 1797 the celebration was banned by the Holy Roman Empire, but it returned for good in 1979, when it was reinstated by the Italian government in an aim to revive the history and culture of Venice. The costumes and masks recall a type of Italian folk street theater called *commedia dell'arte*. The main theme of Carnival changes each year, and people prepare their costumes to fit the theme.

The focal point of the events is Saint Mark's Square, where masqueraders congregate in dazzling costumes. The traditional inauguration of Carnival, the Flight of the Angel, takes place there: an acrobat descends from the bell tower, commemorating a similar daring feat made by a Turkish acrobat in the sixteenth century. People in costumes also take part in boat parades.

The hallmark of this Carnival is the masks. Each day, a competition is held for the most beautiful mask. Winning is a huge honor. In the past, the masks and costumes allowed people to hide their identity. During the celebrations, everyone could be on the same level—rich and poor, princes and merchants. The production of the masks was carried out by a specific guild of artisans called *mascherari*. The masks were made of leather, clay, papier-mâché, and glass, then painted and decorated with baubles, lace, and feathers.

The workshops of these traditional artisans still exist today. Some of the masks they create are based on those used in the performances of old: the Colombina, for example, is a mask decorated with gold, silver, and feathers that covers only the upper

part of the face. The Arlecchino Harlequin is a simple black mask worn with a jester's costume covered in colorful triangles. The Pantalone is a mask of an old man with a long nose, while the Dottore has a long, birdlike beak, mimicking the masks worn long ago by doctors fighting the plague. Another traditional Venetian mask is the square-shaped Bauta, which covers the entire face with no hole for the mouth. It is worn with a triangular hat and a cape. The Volto is a white mask with no expression, and is also worn with a triangular hat.

The first Sunday of Carnival is the Festival of the Marias. Twelve women are chosen from among the residents of the city. Dressed in elaborate costumes, they are carried in a joyful procession to Saint Mark's Square. This commemorates an event from the tenth century, when—according to legend—pirates kidnapped twelve girls from a celebration. The locals managed to defeat the pirates and rescue the girls, and a holiday was announced by the doge, the chief magistrate of Venice.

Traditionally, the girls selected for the parade were provided with a dowry by wealthy families and the doge himself. But today, the celebration is more about admiring the costumes and remembering Venetian tradition.

Carnival of Oruro

Dancing devils and archangels, the Virgin Mary and Mother Earth, a riot of dazzling costumes, and a fabulously colorful, dancing musical fiesta in which ancient beliefs intertwine with Christian traditions—all of this can be found in the Bolivian city of Oruro, whose carnival is included on UNESCO's Representative List of the Intangible Cultural Heritage of Humanity.

Oruro, which is the Hispanicized spelling of Uru Uru, has always been a very important place of worship for the Indigenous Andean peoples. The Uru people had a celebration called Ito, in which they paid homage to their god Pachamama ("Mother Earth") and the ruler of the underworld, Tiw (sometimes called Supay). In the sixteenth century, the area of present-day Bolivia was invaded by the Spanish. The Spanish colonizers set up silver mines in the region and forced the Indigenous people to work there. Tiw, now more commonly called El Tío ("Uncle" in Spanish), was also the god of the mountains and the possessor of minerals, so he became known as the patron and defender of the miners, who sought his favor and protection. To this day, the mines are full of shrines dedicated to El Tío, where workers make offerings to ensure their safety—even if they are Christian.

The Spanish did not like the beliefs of the Indigenous people and banned the celebration of Ito. So the Uru people disguised their customs, pretending that they were celebrating Catholic holidays. This is how traditions began to mix: over time, Pachamama came to be identified with the Virgin Mary, and El Tío with the devil.

Nowadays, the Carnival of Oruro is dedicated to Our Lady of the Mine Shaft (La Virgen del Socavón)—the patron saint of the city, who is also considered the protector of miners. The chapel named after her is a pilgrimage site. The carnival lasts over a week, with the main celebrations beginning on the Saturday before Ash Wednesday. During this time, an extraordinary, all-day procession takes place, attended by thousands of dancers and musicians. The procession route is two and a half miles long. That might not seem like much, but the parade travels this route several times throughout the day. Moreover, it is no ordinary march: the groups perform dance steps, which in some cases have gone unchanged for many, many years. They wear costumes that are often heavy and include fur and masks. These costumes, decorated with embroidery and sequins, are handmade by local craftspeople. In many cases, this profession is passed down from generation to generation. As soon as the carnival ends, preparation begins for the next year's costumes.

Up to thirty thousand dancers, ten thousand musicians, and over four hundred thousand members of the public gather to take part in this fantastic event. The dance groups represent and are inspired by various social and ethnic groups (for example, the

enslaved Africans brought by the Spanish colonizers to work in the mines) and present stories and traditional dances. One of the most important is the Diablada, the Dance of the Devils, symbolizing the fight of good against evil, and dedicated to El Tío. The dance features a colorful procession of devils prancing around the Christian archangel Michael as he fights with Lucifer.

There are stands for the audience along the procession route. The onlookers have other opportunities for entertainment, too, because the carnival is accompanied by a water fight. Plentiful water guns, water balloons, and spray foam ensure that hardly anyone escapes a soaking. There's only one rule: don't spray water on the procession participants!

Purim

Have you ever tried to drive away evil with laughter? That's what happens during Purim. This holiday, the most joyful in the Jewish calendar, is accompanied by commotion, noise, and a procession of celebratory figures in costumes. This is how Jews rejoice at being saved from the cruel fate planned for them by a wicked vizier—his actions symbolically thwarted by the expression of joy.

The Hebrew word *purim* means "lots." It relates not to a quantity, but to a lottery—so Purim is the Feast of Lots. The explanation for this can be found in the book of Esther, the only book in the Bible in which the name of God is not mentioned (for Christians, it is part of the Old Testament). It tells the story of King Ahasuerus, who reigned in Persia and Medea in the second century BCE. His vizier, or adviser, named Haman, convinced the king that the Jews living in his country were not obeying the king's laws, and that this situation must be remedied. Haman came up with a brutal plan—he wanted to kill all the Jews. He drew lots to decide the date his plan would be enacted: the fifteenth day of the month of Adar. This news greatly upset Queen Esther, who was Jewish herself, but who had hidden her origins from the king. For three days she fasted and prayed, considering what to do. Finally, she stood before the ruler, risking severe punishment. Appearing before the king without being summoned was forbidden, even for his wife. In the end, Esther managed to convince Ahasuerus of Haman's wickedness. The Jewish people were saved, and Haman was put to death because of his deceitful scheming.

The day Purim is celebrated depends on the location, but it is either on the fourteenth or fifteenth of Adar (February or March in the Gregorian calendar). Purim is preceded by a one-day fast—Taanit Esther, the Fast of Esther—which lasts from dawn until dusk, but it is not required of everyone, particularly those who are pregnant, nursing, or ill. During the holiday, the book of Esther, which in the Jewish tradition takes the form of a scroll, is read out in synagogues. According to custom, whenever Haman's name is mentioned, it should be drowned out. People stomp enthusiastically and make noise with rattles, whistles, and clappers.

Traditional treats for this holiday include triangular cookies known in Hebrew as *oznei Haman*, or "Haman's ears," and in Yiddish as *hamantaschen*, or "Haman's pockets." The cookies are stuffed with poppy seeds, dried fruits, or jam. People also eat other sweet treats and give them out as gifts to friends in special baskets called *mishloach manot* that families often make at home.

Charity is an extremely important element of Purim, so various charity balls and collections are organized. It is customary to make donations to those in need, which should amount to the equivalent of two meals. Traditionally, alms were given in the form of three half-shekel coins because the word *terumah*, which means "an offering," was mentioned three times when God explained to the prophet Moses how Israelites should make donations.

In Jewish communities, Purim is celebrated as a carnival. Parties are held in the streets, DJs play music, and people dance in costumes ranging from kings and queens

to superheroes and book characters. In ancient times, masqueraders would playfully reenact the story of Esther, Ahasuerus, and the evil Haman. Children would go from house to house, acting out Purim scenes in exchange for small amounts of money and candy. They would also make comedic speeches, often referring to current events, and recite humorous poems.

These Purim spiels (derived from the Yiddish word for "play"), which still take place today, are comic dramatizations of the book of Esther that explain Purim and why it is celebrated.

All Saints' and All Souls' Day

In late autumn, darkness falls quickly in the northern hemisphere. Cemeteries are usually locked after dark. But in some parts of the world during these holidays, the gates remain open all night and the cemeteries are illuminated with an extraordinary glow: the flames of hundreds of candles, placed on the graves to honor the memory of deceased loved ones.

The first day of November is All Saints' Day, when the Christian church commemorates believers who were recognized as saints after death or whose lives were particularly pious. The second is All Souls' Day. It is a celebration of all departed souls, especially those close to us. For Christians, these days are associated with a belief in resurrection, and prayers are said for souls who are repenting for bad deeds. People who don't observe religion may also light candles at graves as a sign of remembrance

In the past, fires were lit near cemeteries and at crossroads to protect against various demonic beings, but also to allow wandering spirits to warm up, and to light their way to the spirit world. On All Souls' Day, flames were commonly placed at the graves of people who had died suddenly, because it was thought that their souls could get lost on earth. It was also believed that on this night the dead could return to their homes. People would leave their doors ajar and put out meals. To this day, in Slovakia people leave out refreshments on All Souls' Day. In the past, people in Poland, Lithuania, and Belarus also held a ceremony called Dziady, during which spirits were summoned to participate in a feast.

The custom of lighting lamps or bringing flowers to graves is also common in countries such as Germany. In France, instead of lights, people leave flowers, wreaths, and cards with written memories of the deceased. Speaking of flowers, in Poland, All Souls' Day is associated with chrysanthemums and lilies.

In Austria, Seleenwoche (All Souls' Week) is celebrated between October 30 and November 8. People display lights in their homes and leave out bread and water to welcome any dead souls back to Earth. Lamps are taken to the graves on November 1.

Christians in the Philippines might celebrate All Souls' Day through the whole night. Graves are decorated with flowers and candles as well as balloons and ribbons. Entire families gather at the cemeteries. They often stay overnight—they pitch tents, eat, play cards or dice, and watch shows and videos. It's as if they're spending time with the dead. This custom is reminiscent of the Mexican Día de los Muertos.

Halloween

In most English-speaking countries, on the night of October 31—All Hallows' Eve—witches, ghosts, vampires, and skeletons come out to play. Houses are decorated with lanterns made from hollowed-out pumpkins carved with shapes and images as well as symbols of fear—ghosts, cobwebs, spiders, and skulls. Children dressed in costumes go from house to house calling out, "Trick or treat!" to ask for candy.

Halloween arrived in the United States thanks to Irish immigrants, although many people think of it as an American holiday. This belief probably comes from the ubiquity of Halloween in pop culture; due to American movies and TV series, this holiday has reached many countries around the world. In fact, American customs have influenced how Halloween is celebrated in Ireland and the United Kingdom today.

Researchers have various theories about the origins of this tradition. Some think it derived from the Celtic festival of Samhain, which signals the end of the harvest and the beginning of winter: a period of darkness and hunger. It was believed that on Samhain, the boundary between the world of the living and the spirit world became thin, allowing the dead to cross over. The druids, ancient Celtic priests, would put on black costumes and masks made of rutabaga and turnips carved to resemble demonic faces. These masks were supposed to protect against evil spirits.

The hollowed-out pumpkin is called a jack-o'-lantern. In the past, this term was also used to refer to a man with a lantern, such as a watchman, or a will-o'-the-wisp. The custom of making lanterns is associated with a folk legend about Jack, of which there are numerous versions. Jack is said to have been a cunning man who outsmarted the devil and then found his way through the spirit world, lighting his way with a hollowed-out turnip containing a coal he received from the devil. Over time, the turnip was replaced with a pumpkin, but one thing remained unchanged: the lantern served to light the way for lost souls.

The tradition of walking from house to house dressed in disguises dates back many centuries; in the past, it was often the poor who went around asking for donations and food. The contemporary custom of trick-or-treating became popular in the United States and Canada in the twentieth century, then began to spread to other countries like the United Kingdom and Ireland. Previous generations tend to remember lighting fires, telling scary stories, and various tricks played on neighbors and family.

Another tradition associated with Halloween is bobbing for apples, a game where players fish an apple out of a bucket of water using only their teeth. Themed costume parties are also popular, and those who particularly like to be scared participate in horror movie marathons or visit haunted houses.

Día de los Muertos

This Mexican holiday is not a time for melancholy or reflection. It pulses with color, music, even laughter. Everywhere you look, there are flowers, candles, elaborate shrines, sugar skulls, and masquerades of dancing skeletons. Día de los Muertos is about more than death—it's a time for strengthening family ties.

Mexicans who observe the holiday believe that the dead can pay them visits at this time of year. Therefore, this is a joyful holiday, a chance to welcome your loved ones who have passed away. Such special guests should be treated appropriately, and fulfilling this obligation ensures the protection of the house and its inhabitants. The guests from the spirit world are encouraged with special altars called *ofrendas*—these can be located in people's homes or in public places, such as shops, offices, or gas stations.

The most traditional type of altar consists of seven steps symbolizing the seven levels the soul goes through after death. Often the altars have just three or four steps, which get smaller toward the top of the altar. Items are placed on the altar in a specific order: food and drink (especially dishes and drinks that the person liked when they were alive), salt (for protection and cleansing), incense, a photo of the deceased, images of saints and the Virgin Mary, and a cross. Other elements include flowers (orange marigolds, called *cempasúchil* in Mexico, are dedicated to the dead); skulls made of sugar or chocolate (the sugar is supposed to give energy to the souls); candles; cutouts made of colorful crepe paper, called *papel picado*; maize, which is associated with the harvest; sugarcane; fruit, as a gift from nature; a vessel of water; and a special sweet yeast bread called *pan de muerto*, or "bread of the dead." Various things that the person loved when they were alive are also placed on the altar—for example, a favorite book for an avid reader, or a prized instrument for a musician. The exact selection of items depends on the specific region and home. Altars are erected not only for loved ones but also for historical figures, respected artists, and sometimes literary and film figures.

Tombstones are also decorated at this time with flowers, sugar skulls, and candies. The sounds of music and partying can be heard drifting from the cemetery all night long. Many relatives play recorded music to liven up their family gatherings, but live mariachi bands playing traditional folk music are also common sightings. However, the essence of the celebrations is remembrance—by recalling what the deceased person was like and what they loved, and by preparing their favorite dishes, the family can feel that they are close during the holiday.

In some regions of Mexico, on Día de los Muertos people dress up as La Catrina, a skeleton woman with painted cheeks who wears an elegant dress and hat. Her image was created in the early twentieth century by the printmaker José Guadalupe Posada, and she owes her name to another famous Mexican artist, Diego Rivera. Originally, she was a satirical figure—a mockery of the women who denied their Indigenous

ancestry by powdering their faces and delighting in European fashions. Nowadays, she is a symbol of death. But no one is afraid of La Catrina, or of the dancing skeletons, because Mexicans consider death a normal part of life. Skulls decorated with ornaments, walking skeletons with big grins, and of course La Catrina are reminders of the inevitability of death, but in a cheerful form, which is easier to come to terms with.

Some people believe that Día de los Muertos combines Christian customs with the three-thousand-year-old traditions of Indigenous peoples such as the Aztecs, Tarascans, Mayans, and Totonacs. Before the arrival of the Spanish colonizers, a celebration during what is now known as August lasted almost a month and was linked to the end of the growing season and the harvest period. Maize and beans were particularly important crops. The holiday was dedicated to Mictlantecuhtli, the Aztec god of death, and his wife, Mictecacihuatl. It was moved to November to link it with the Christian All Saints' Day. Since then, November 2 has marked the most important celebrations dedicated to adults who have died. The day before is a day of memory for children who have died, and the altars are decorated with flowers and toys.

The celebration of Día de los Muertos is included on UNESCO's Representative List of the Intangible Cultural Heritage of Humanity.

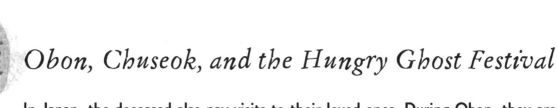

Obon, Chuseok, and the Hungry Ghost Festival

In Japan, the deceased also pay visits to their loved ones. During Obon, they are invited as guests, offered food and drink, and then helped to find their way back to the spirit world.

Obon lasts for three days. The holiday has been celebrated for over five hundred years, but because Japan has changed calendars in this time, the starting date of Obon varies in different parts of the country (although it is mainly in August in the Gregorian calendar). Many Japanese people take time off during this holiday to return to their hometowns. On the first day, people visit cemeteries. They clean the graves, decorate them with flowers, and light incense. When they return home, they carry lanterns to show the spirits the way. Lanterns are also hung in people's homes, and small "welcoming fires" called *mukaebi* are sometimes lit in front of doorways.

People set up altars at home with candles and pictures of their deceased ancestors, and lay out fruit, water, and sweets—although this is not only for Obon. Family members gather there to pray. Cucumbers and eggplants often feature among the offerings, but these are not snacks for the spirits. Pieces of cucumber are assembled and carved to look like a horse, and eggplant to look like a cow. The horse is supposed to swiftly carry ancestors to meet their waiting relatives, and the cow will take them back to the spirit world.

On the third day of the holiday, it's time to say goodbye to the visiting souls and wish them a good journey back to the spirit world. People accompany them to the cemetery carrying lanterns. In some places, people take special lanterns to the water—the ocean or a river. They are released with the current in a ceremony called Tōrō Nagashi. Small *okuribi*, "farewell fires," are lit outside houses, and large ones on hilltops.

The deceased are honored with the *bon odori*, a dance composed of rhythmic, repetitive movements. The particular steps vary depending on the region and might convey stories or local history, or relate to certain customs. The dancers are usually dressed in traditional summer *yukata* robes and dance around a raised stage, called a *yagura*, accompanied by live music. This is mainly classical Japanese music and folk tunes, but can include contemporary songs too. The movements are not very complicated, so the people watching the show can join in the dancing. The mood is cheerful, depicting the joy of visits from deceased loved ones.

In other parts of Asia, the spirits are also tended with offerings of food and drink, or shown the way with lanterns.

In South Korea, the dead are honored during Chuseok, a three-day harvest festival falling on the fifteenth day of the eighth lunar month (September or October in the Gregorian calendar). People prepare a table full of dishes arranged according to specific rules. The dishes are dedicated to the ancestors, and then eaten by the whole family at a shared meal. (This ceremonial table is also featured during the celebration of Seollal, Korean New Year.) During Chuseok, people visit cemeteries to clean the graves and remove the grass that has grown over the summer. As a mark of respect, it's traditional to bow in front of the graves. Younger family members must offer two bows for the deceased. Since they should only offer one bow for the living family elders, it's important not to mix these up!

The seventh month of the Chinese lunar calendar sees the celebration of the Hungry Ghost Festival in southern China, Malaysia, Singapore, Hong Kong, and Taiwan. This is considered the time when the spirits of people without living relatives to take care of them roam the earth. To help look after these spirits, people set up altars with food and drinks, and send the spirits items they might need or want in the spirit world, including money, clothes, and TVs—this is done by burning paper images of the items. The needs of relatives living in the spirit world are met in the same way. As you might remember, paper money is also burned at Chinese New Year.

It is believed that spirits like artistic performances, which is why the front row is often left free for them at traditional Chinese operas during the Hungry Ghost Festival. Throughout the Ghost Month, superstitious people avoid various activities, like buying a car or new home, to not attract bad luck.

In China, deceased loved ones are honored with the Qingming ("Pure Brightness") Festival, also known as Tomb-Sweeping Day. It falls on the fifteenth day after the spring equinox. On this day, family members visit the graves of relatives to clean them and offer food, drink, and burned money. Wreaths are laid, and family members make a ceremonial bow. Sometimes people also bring a willow branch—according to folk beliefs, this is meant to drive away evil spirits.

Saint Lucy's Day

On December 13 in Sweden, a ceremonial procession takes place. Singing children dressed in white robes carry lights, led by a girl with a wreath on her head. The wreath contains candles and resembles a luminous crown. The celebrations are held in memory of a Christian saint.

According to legend, Saint Lucy lived in ancient Rome. As a young girl, she is said to have brought meals to Christians who were trapped in the catacombs, and she lit her way in the dark with candles woven into her wreath. Why wear candles on her head? So that she could carry as much food as possible in both hands.

This is a very sad story, because at that time, Christians in Rome were persecuted. Lucy refused to renounce her faith and was executed in 304 CE. Today, however, this occasion is celebrated with joy. Families sit down together for dinner and eat delicious yeast buns flavored with saffron. They are called *lussekatter*, meaning "Lucy cats." Each bun is shaped like the letter S, but also looks a little like a sleeping cat, an animal that used to be connected with the devil. But thanks to the bright yellow from the saffron, which represents light, the treats are thought to ward off the devil.

The holiday falls when the nights in this part of the world are at their longest. Therefore, darkness is dispelled with light. The candles also symbolize waiting for spring and people's joy that the daytime and light will soon arrive. The Latin word for light is *lux*, and the name Lucy comes from this word.

This day is also celebrated in other Scandinavian countries, where winter is long and dark. The Caribbean island of Saint Lucia, which is named after Saint Lucy, celebrates this as their National Day with lantern presentations and a fireworks display.

Historical Events

Around the world, there are many holidays marking important dates from the past, or remembering particular leaders. These are not always happy celebrations—sometimes they commemorate sad or dramatic events.

June 16 is Youth Day in South Africa. This might sound like a joyful occasion, but it actually commemorates the brutal incidents of 1976. In the town of Soweto near Johannesburg, protests were held against apartheid—the racist government policy that discriminated against Black residents—and violently suppressed by the police. Students were demanding education at a better level and in their own languages; the government wanted to impose teaching in Afrikaans, the language of the white Afrikaner people. Many young people were shot, including twelve-year-old Hector Pieterson. A monument was erected at the site of his death to honor the youth fighting against apartheid. In 1991, the Organization of African Unity, in collaboration with UNICEF, assigned June 16 as the International Day of the African Child to draw the world's attention to the problems that children in Africa face, such as lack of adequate health care, high mortality, unequal treatment of girls and boys, and lack of access to education.

For many countries that have not always been independent, the anniversary of gaining independence is an occasion for joyful celebrations. In the United States, Independence Day is celebrated on July 4—on this day in 1776, the American colonists announced their independence from Great Britain. There are numerous parades, fireworks displays, concerts, and festivals.

Independence Day is also commemorated in India (August 15), Pakistan (August 14), and over one hundred countries that gained independence, usually after years of colonial rule by European countries.

In Poland, on November 11 people celebrate the anniversary of regaining

freedom in 1918, after 123 years of control by neighboring countries. Special concerts and parades take place, and many people hang Polish flags in their windows.

In New Zealand—also known by its Māori name, Aotearoa—Waitangi Day is celebrated on February 6 to commemorate the signing of the Treaty of Waitangi in 1840 between representatives of Māori tribes and the British authorities. Under this treaty, the Māori people—previously discriminated against by the colonizers—were granted civil rights as well as the right to own land and other goods. The Treaty of Waitangi is considered the founding document of modern New Zealand. Waitangi Day celebrations include shows and presentations about Māori culture, including music, dance, and food.

In Norway, one of the most important national holidays is Constitution Day, celebrated on May 17. The day commemorates when the Constitution of Norway was signed in 1814, declaring Norway as an independent kingdom. In the capital,

Oslo, students parade in front of the Royal Palace, where they are greeted by the monarch. People of all ages go out into the streets with flags, dressed in traditional national outfits. On that day, walking the city streets can feel like being at a folklore festival.

On April 23, Turkey celebrates Ulusal Egemenlik ve Çocuk Bayramı, "National Sovereignty and Children's Day." In addition to commemorating the establishment of the Turkish parliament in 1920, this holiday also honors children as a sign that they're the ones who determine the country's future. Students decorate their classrooms and organize parties, and concerts and parades are held.

In Germany, October 3 is German Unity Day, commemorating the 1990 unification of the eastern and western parts of the country after thirty years of division. More than the reunification of the country, the celebration focuses on the unity and solidarity of its citizens.

Another celebration of unity—not of a country this time, but of an entire continent—is marked in Africa on May 25. Africa Day commemorates the establishment in 1963 of the Organization of African Unity (later transformed into the African Union), which focuses on the development of African countries following the many fights for independence and political rights in African nations after years of European colonial rule.

The most important date in the French calendar is Bastille Day, which falls on July 14. It commemorates the storming of the Bastille prison in 1789, the start of the French Revolution, which resulted in the people overthrowing the absolute monarchy. Nowadays, Bastille Day celebrations feature fireworks and military parades.

Juneteenth, celebrated on June 19, marks the end of slavery in the United States. It was on this day in 1865, two years after slavery was officially abolished, that the news finally reached enslaved African Americans in Texas. This occasion is celebrated with picnics and festivals featuring music, food, and dancing, as well as educational meetings and discussion panels recognizing the ongoing struggles of Black Americans, who were long deprived of their civil rights. For a long time, Juneteenth was celebrated only in some states, but in 2021 the federal government passed a resolution making it a nationwide holiday.

Some events are celebrated in many countries, such as the end of World War I on November 11, 1918. In some countries, this is called Armistice Day in commemoration of the peace, or Remembrance Day to remember those who died in the war. In the United States, this day is called Veterans Day to honor all veterans, not just those who served in World War I.

Some countries have holidays to honor specific rulers. In Bhutan, December 17 is National Day, marking the date the current dynasty began its rule in 1907. The monarch's birthday is also an occasion for celebration: parades take place and students prepare various performances.

Speaking of royal birthdays, in the United Kingdom the birthday of the monarch has been celebrated in June since the seventeenth century. The official birthday falls

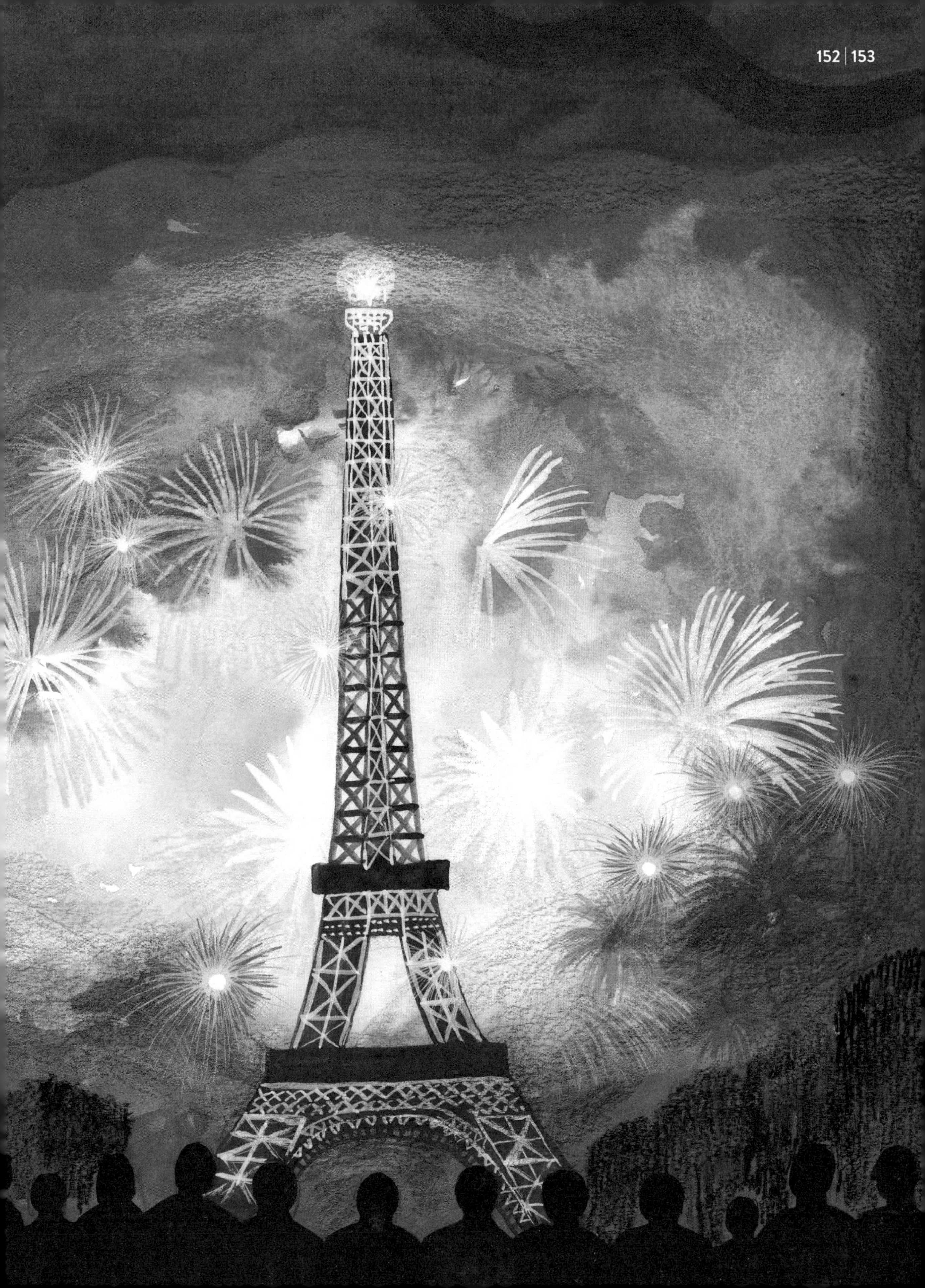

at the same time of year for every British monarch, regardless of when they were actually born—supposedly, this decision was made by King George II, who was born in the autumn, when the weather in England can be quite dreary, and he didn't think it was a good time for a celebration. Since 1748 the official birthdays have been marked by a unique military parade known as Trooping the Colour, in which the King's (or Queen's) Guard march in their distinctive red uniforms and tall black hats. Every year the show attracts crowds of spectators, who watch it from the stands lining the parade route.

Although it is not a traditional calendar holiday, in many countries around the world June is declared Pride Month. It is dedicated to LGBTQ+ people who face discrimination, aggression, and exclusion in everyday life, even from their loved ones, and who have to fight for their rights. The name refers both to pride in oneself and to living without hiding or feeling ashamed. Events during Pride focus on tolerance and equality, creativity, and LGBTQ+ public figures, signaling their presence in society. Parades are also organized, with participants carrying rainbow flags and colorful banners. The original six-colored rainbow flag representing the LGBTQ+ community is a joyful symbol of hope and reconciliation, and there are now numerous variations of it to represent specific groups within the community.

Pride Month originated in the United States as a commemoration of the events of June 28, 1969, in New York, when the police made an unjustified raid on the Stonewall Inn, one of the few gay bars at the time. The bar's customers, fed up with being treated like criminals and discriminated against, clashed with the police, and a riot broke out. These events are considered the symbolic beginning of the movement for LGBTQ+ equality in the United States.

We have looked at public holidays celebrated across entire continents and in individual countries. But there are also holidays that are observed in smaller communities, neighborhoods, towns, or villages. It's worth checking whether a special occasion is celebrated in your town or even on your street.

Saint Patrick's Day

In Ireland, March 17—when the Christian church commemorates Saint Patrick on the day of his death—has become more than a date in the religious calendar. It is also a national holiday, but it's not a serious or sad occasion. The Irish (whether they are religious or not) celebrate the traditions of their homeland with great enthusiasm. The holiday has also become popular in many other places around the world, especially where there are communities of people with Irish ancestry.

Green, the traditional color of Ireland and Saint Patrick, is inextricably linked with the celebrations. People dress in green clothes, and old buildings and monuments are illuminated with green lights. In Chicago, the river is even dyed green! The three-leaf clover, or shamrock—the symbol of Ireland—is everywhere. According to legend, Patrick used a shamrock to explain to people the idea of the Holy Trinity: Christians believe that there is one God, but that he exists in three forms: the Father, the Son, and the Holy Spirit.

But who was Saint Patrick? His birth name was Maewyn Succat, and he was born about 1,600 years ago in Britain, where he lived until he was captured by Irish raiders as a teenager. In Ireland, he was enslaved and forced to work as a shepherd. Finally, he managed to escape, and after numerous adventures he returned home. He became a priest and took the Latin name Patricius, but was commonly known as Pádraig or Patrick. Despite the bad memories, he returned to Ireland, where he taught people about his faith.

In Dublin (the capital of the Republic of Ireland) and in other places around the world, the celebration of Saint Patrick's Day is accompanied by a large parade with marching bands, people in costumes, and various themed floats. Of course green predominates, but there is also plenty of white and orange to represent the three colors of the Irish flag. Folk music concerts and traditional Irish dance shows are organized. Some people dress up as a leprechaun—a character from folk legends, a mischievous elf with a red beard, a green jacket, and a tall hat. It's worth keeping an eye out for the leprechaun, because he's said to have hidden a pot of gold at the end of the rainbow!

Kodomo no Hi

Colorful carp are flapping in the air. Yes, you read that right: carp. But these particular fish don't need water to swim in, because they are *koinobori*, streamers made of fabric or paper. They look like they're swimming in the wind! People in Japan hang the fish outside their homes on May 5 to celebrate Kodomo no Hi, or "Children's Day."

This day wasn't always dedicated to all children—originally, it was Tango no Sekku (Boys' Day), and even earlier it was a completely different, agricultural holiday associated with the blooming of irises. Girls still have a separate special day, Hinamatsuri (Doll Festival), which falls on March 3. However, this is not a public holiday, while Kodomo no Hi was proclaimed as such by the Japanese government when it was established for all children in 1948.

Due to the holiday's history, many of the customs related to Children's Day are more stereotypically boy-focused. For example, people put up home displays of miniature warrior dolls wearing armor, with swords or bows. The displays reflect parents' desire for their children to be healthy and strong. Samurai dolls are important

in celebrating Kodomo no Hi, and one of the mythical heroes whose image is often represented in doll form is Kintarō. According to legend, he was a boy with super-human powers. Kintarō was raised by mountain witches and became friendly with animals. He performed many extraordinary deeds, and characters inspired by him often appear in manga, anime, and Japanese video games.

Because the dolls are expensive and space is needed to display them, sometimes families just display a *kabuto*, a miniature samurai helmet. A popular activity for both boys and girls is folding paper origami helmets. Martial arts shows are also organized for the occasion of Kodomo no Hi.

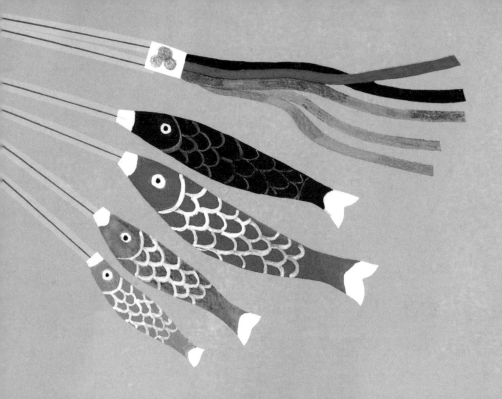

In the past, only families with sons would display *koinobori*, but now any family can take part in the custom. Different colors of carp symbolize the members of the family: Black is the father. Red is the mother. The others, smaller and in different colors, are the children. Not everyone has space to display large streamers, so some people put up miniature *koinobori* as decorations inside the house. And why carp? Because they are associated with steadfastness, strength, and the determination needed to ensure success. This is influenced by Chinese culture, and the belief that a carp that swims up the Yellow River and then jumps through the Dragon Gate at the top of the waterfall flowing down from the legendary Longmen Mountains will transform into a dragon and be taken to heaven.

An older tradition, beautifully fragrant, dates back to the times of the ancient agricultural festival: hanging irises and mugwort on the eaves of houses to scare away evil forces and bring health and prosperity. Bathing in water with irises is said to have cleansing powers. On Kodomo no Hi, public baths offer these special flower baths, and children can sometimes use them for free.

Of course, there are also many special delicacies for this occasion. Among the most popular treats are *kashiwa mochi*—chewy rice cakes stuffed with sweet red-bean paste and served on oak leaves. The oak symbolizes the health of one's family and ancestors, since the indigenous oak trees don't shed their old leaves until new leaves grow. Another specialty is *chimaki*—long, cone-shaped dumplings made of sticky rice wrapped in bamboo leaves and steamed.

The miniature samurai of Kodomo no Hi probably became part of the older Boys' Day thanks to the influence of the "girly" Hinamatsuri. During Hinamatsuri, people display sets of dolls in their homes. The dolls, called *hina ningyō*, are dressed in historical costumes from the Heian period. At least two dolls should be displayed, representing the emperor and empress in front of a golden screen, but in its full version the exhibition consists of a multilevel platform with several additional figurines depicting ladies of the court, ministers, musicians, and guards.

As well as the dolls, various accessories and decorations can be added, such as miniature cherry and tangerine trees. As far as possible, *hina ningyō* are passed down from generation to generation. If no inherited dolls are available in a family, the girl receives a set from her grandparents or parents for her first Hinamatsuri, and other elements of *hina ningyō* are also donated by family members. Unfortunately, these dolls aren't for playing with: they're just a decoration. The display is put up about two weeks before the date of the holiday and should be dismantled three days after. Superstitious people believe that if the display isn't taken down, the girl won't find a partner when she grows up.

On Hinamatsuri, girls get together for parties. They enjoy sweet treats, which they first offer symbolically to the dolls. Just like at Kodomo no Hi, there are rice-based delicacies, including mochi. There are also savory dishes, such as *ushio-jiru*, a clear clam soup. Sweet, nonalcoholic sake is also served.

Thanksgiving

This is the most family-focused of the US and Canadian holidays. For many people who live far away from their families, it may be their only opportunity during the year to get together with loved ones. On the fourth Thursday of November in the United States (the second Monday of October in Canada), families and friends sit down together at a table laden with food and drink, adorned with autumnal decorations, and (usually) dominated by a giant turkey. Just as important as meeting and eating is giving thanks—many people say what they are grateful for and thank others for various things.

In 1863, President Abraham Lincoln proclaimed Thanksgiving a public holiday in the United States. Although it draws from religious traditions, it is secular in nature and celebrated by people regardless of faith. It is generally believed to have its basis in stories about early British settlers, known as Pilgrims, who were fleeing religious persecution in England in the seventeenth century and arrived in America on board the *Mayflower*. Their ship landed on the coast of present-day Massachusetts in 1620, and the new arrivals built a settlement they named Plymouth. It was a difficult first year: the harsh winter brought famine, and almost half of the more than one hundred settlers died. Luckily, the pilgrims were helped by the Indigenous Wampanoag people. The following year's successful harvest was celebrated with a great feast shared by the settlers and the Wampanoag people. But while the holiday takes its inspiration from principles of mutual agreement and multiethnicity, the subsequent history of America strayed far from these ideals.

These days, the Thanksgiving table typically includes turkey, gravy, and stuffing—which can be baked and served separately—as well as pumpkin pie, cranberry sauce, and mashed potatoes. But each home might have its own dishes, drawing from different cultural traditions. Amid the festive, family atmosphere, many people also like to watch football on TV.

Not all turkeys end up in the oven on Thanksgiving. For many years now, there has been a tradition that the president of the United States ceremonially "pardons" a selected bird on the Tuesday before Thanksgiving. The lucky turkey spends the rest of its life on a farm in Virginia, having stayed for the night before the ceremony in a luxury hotel.

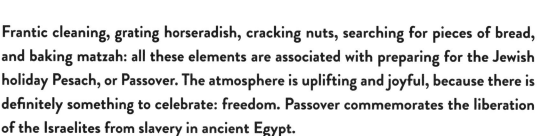

Passover

Frantic cleaning, grating horseradish, cracking nuts, searching for pieces of bread, and baking matzah: all these elements are associated with preparing for the Jewish holiday Pesach, or Passover. The atmosphere is uplifting and joyful, because there is definitely something to celebrate: freedom. Passover commemorates the liberation of the Israelites from slavery in ancient Egypt.

The highlight of this important holiday is the retelling of the story of the liberation of the Israelites. According to the Bible, the cruel ruler Pharaoh enslaved the Israelites living in his country. Commanded by God to save his people, Moses asked Pharaoh to let them go. Each time Pharaoh refused, God would send a severe plague to Egypt. The last plague was the most terrible—the death of the firstborn sons. However, it did not affect the Israelites, because God warned them through Moses, ordering them to smear the blood of a sacrificed lamb on the doors and thresholds of their homes so the Angel of Death would "pass over" them. Finally, Moses was able to lead the Israelites out of Egypt, across the Red Sea—which was parted by the power of God—and through the desert.

Religious Jews prepare for Passover by cleaning their houses very thoroughly, from the basement to the attic, to remove all traces of *chametz*—foods made from cereals such as rye, wheat, spelt, oats, and barley, and risen dough, such as bread. To get rid of the remains of *chametz*, they can sell it to someone who is not Jewish (a good idea if there's too much to throw away) or burn it. Families make a special Passover game out of the cleaning. On the evening before the holiday, one family member hides ten pieces of bread around the house. The rest of the family has to find them. The search takes place with the lights off, using a candle or a flashlight to make it more fun. Once the pieces of bread are located, they are traditionally swept with a bird's feather onto a wooden spoon and then placed in a paper bag. Finally, the feather and spoon are placed in the bag as well and a declaration is made: there is no *chametz* left in the house, and if any remains despite the family's efforts, let it turn to dust. The following day, a few hours before the holiday begins, the remaining *chametz* must be burned.

During the week of Passover, utensils that have been in contact with *chametz* should not be used unless they are specially cleaned in accordance with *kashrut*, the rules that define what Jews can and cannot eat and how food should be stored. When possible, religious families have a completely separate set of tableware for Passover. In place of the forbidden *chametz*, people eat matzah, a flat cracker-like bread baked especially for this holiday. It is prepared without any yeast or leavening agent from thinly rolled sheets of dough made only of flour and water. This is a reminder of the escape from Egypt: the Israelites left their homes in such a hurry that the dough for their bread didn't have time to rise.

Passover begins with a special dinner called a seder. Three pieces of matzah are stacked on a plate or napkin and then covered. The three pieces of matzah represent the ancient divisions of Jewish society: the top one is for the priests; the middle one for the Levites, God's servants in the temple; and the bottom one for the rest of the believers.

Also present on the table is a decorated seder plate, with six separate hollows, each for an item with symbolic meaning. One is *beitzah*, a hard-boiled egg baked on the fire, symbolizing the destruction of the Temple of Jerusalem and hope for the coming of the Messiah who will rebuild the temple. Another element is *zeroa*, a piece of bone with a bit of meat roasted on the fire, commemorating the sacrifices made

at the Temple of Jerusalem. This bone is not consumed. *Karpas* is a vegetable, such as parsley, celery, onion, or potato, representing the fact that Passover is a spring holiday and symbolizing liberation. It is eaten after dipping in salt water, signifying the tears shed in captivity. Also found on the seder plate are two bitter vegetables, *maror* and *chazeret* (known as "bitter herbs"): grated horseradish and chicory, endive, or romaine lettuce, which are also eaten after dipping in salt water to commemorate the bitterness of the times of slavery. The bitterness is sweetened with wine, matzah, and sweet *charoset*—a paste the color of clay, symbolizing the clay used by Israelites in captivity to make bricks. *Charoset* is prepared differently in different parts of the world. In one well-known version, it is made from raw grated apple and chopped nuts, and seasoned with wine, cinnamon, and cloves.

During the seder feast, those gathered around the table read the Haggadah, a book—often beautifully illustrated—recounting the story of the Exodus from Egypt. The Haggadah is meant to both engage and entertain, as well as answer important questions about the customs of the holiday itself, such as why bitter herbs and matzah are eaten, and why salt water is used. The ingredients from the seder plate help to tell the story. The Passover seder is especially important for children, as it teaches them about their heritage and helps them learn why this night is different from all others.

The rich ceremony around the seder includes many rituals, blessings, and prayers. The dinner is just one part of it. Not all Jews eat the same foods. During the feast, there is time for other customs, including games and singing. The seder can last long into the night, sometimes even until morning.

Passover begins on the fifteenth day of the Hebrew month of Nisan, which coincides with the first (or second, in certain years) spring full moon. (In the Gregorian calendar, this is late March or April.) Some researchers believe that even before the Exodus of the Israelites from Egypt, a holiday—either an agricultural festival or rite of protection for the family home—was celebrated in nearby areas at this time of year, and that the celebration of Passover merged with these ancient customs. Nowadays, the holiday lasts seven days in Israel or eight days outside Israel, with the most important seder taking place on the first night. The next day, the sixteenth of Nisan, marks the beginning of the public countdown of the *omer*, the forty-nine days remaining until the Jewish holiday of Shavuot, the agricultural "Feast of Weeks."

Dragon Boat Festival

On the fifth day of the fifth month of the Chinese calendar (usually in June), the races begin. Long, slender boats with dragon heads at their prows speed down rivers and across lakes. The sides of the boats, painted with colorful scales or other designs, shimmer in the sun. The paddlers strain to make their dragons the fastest. They are accompanied by drummers, pounding a rhythm, spurring them on. On the shore, excited fans cheer as they snack on *zòngzi* dumplings.

What are the origins of this spectacular custom, which has developed into a national holiday in China and is featured on UNESCO's Representative List of the Intangible Cultural Heritage of Humanity?

It is linked to various legends, one of the most popular being a story about the ancient royal adviser and poet Qu Yuan, who was devoted to his homeland. He lived at a time when China was made up of rival kingdoms constantly at war with one another. Unfortunately, the ruler did not appreciate Qu Yuan's wisdom and ordered him to be exiled from the court. So Qu Yuan lived as a poor man among ordinary people, wrote wistful poems about his love for his lost country, and collected folk stories and songs. One day, when he heard that his homeland had been conquered, he threw himself into a river out of despair. People in boats flocked to rescue him, but to no avail. To prevent the poet's body from being eaten by the river-ruling dragon, the *jiāolóng*, they threw *zòngzi* into the water. According to another version of the legend, the *zòngzi* were thrown into the water so that Qu Yuan's soul wouldn't starve in the afterlife.

But what exactly are *zòngzi*? These dumplings consist of sticky rice formed into a distinctive triangular shape and stuffed with a sweet or savory filling. They are wrapped in bamboo leaves or sometimes banana leaves. The green parcels are tied with string, to prevent them from falling apart, and then steamed.

Dragon boats are just under four feet wide but over forty feet long, and the paddles range in length from around three to four feet. Typically, the crew consists of twenty-two people: twenty paddlers (sitting in pairs on benches, with the first pair setting the pace), a steersperson at the back, who sets the direction with a special long oar, and a drummer at the front. The beautiful dragon heads are detached from the boats during training to prevent them from getting damaged. As well as in China, the holiday is celebrated in Taiwan and Hong Kong. Other countries also organize dragon boat competitions for purely sporting reasons. There are even world championships.

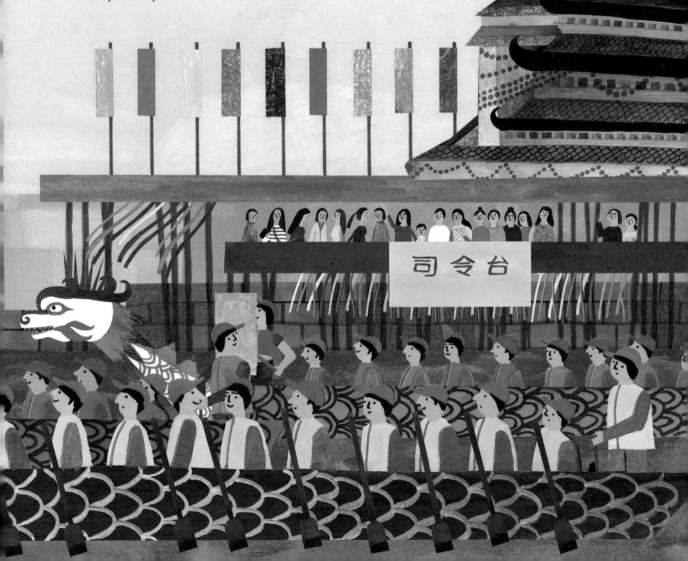

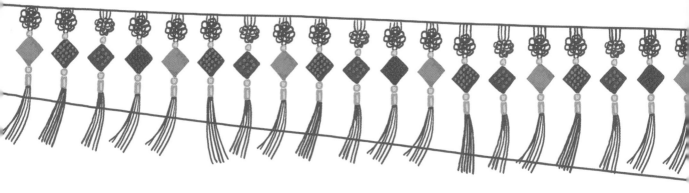

In China, special decorations are made or purchased to celebrate the Dragon Boat Festival: people tie multicolored charm bracelets to their wrists and wear scented sachets to protect against diseases. It is customary to hang calamus and wormwood outside the house to ward off misfortune and evil—and, on a more practical level, insects.

There is also a game associated with the Dragon Boat Festival that involves balancing eggs in an upright position. Egg-balancing competitions are organized in shops and outside temples. It's a game especially enjoyed by children, who also have playful battles to try and break the eggshells of their opponents. All in all, it's an egg-cellent occasion for celebration!

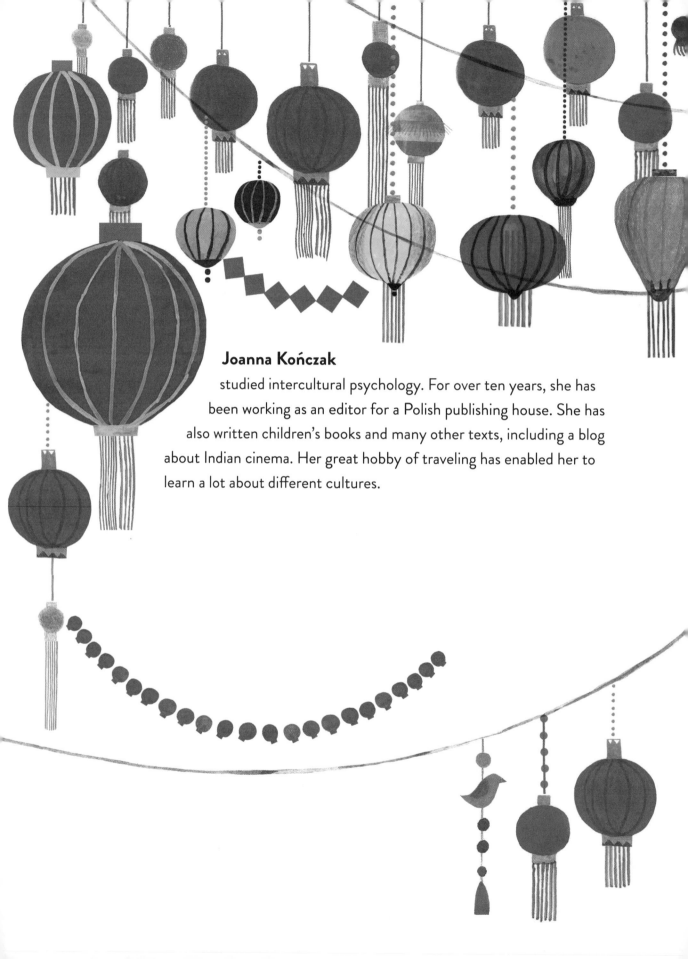

Joanna Kończak

studied intercultural psychology. For over ten years, she has
been working as an editor for a Polish publishing house. She has
also written children's books and many other texts, including a blog
about Indian cinema. Her great hobby of traveling has enabled her to
learn a lot about different cultures.

Ewa
Poklewska-Koziełło

was born and raised in Gdańsk, Poland, where she studied architecture. She loves to paint, especially for children. She has illustrated dozens of books and magazines for children. *Let's Get Festive!* is her second book with NorthSouth.

Christmas is Coming

Traditions from Around the World

978-0-7358-4443-8

The perfect book for long wintry evenings—not just under the Christmas tree!

Why do we decorate Christmas trees? Do all children receive gifts on the same day?

Come find out as Monika Utnik-Strugała captures the smells, tastes, and unforgettable traditions about the most popular, exciting, contemplative, and unique Christmas customs and legends from around the world. Find out why people celebrate Christmas on December 25, who invented the first glass ornament, why people build nativity scenes, and more!

With atmospheric illustrations by Ewa Poklewska-Koziełło, this is an ideal companion for the Christmas season.

Text copyright © 2023 by Joanna Kończak
Illustrations copyright © 2023 by Ewa Poklewska-Koziełło
English translation copyright © 2024 by Kate Webster
First English edition published in 2024 by
NorthSouth Books Inc., New York 10016, an imprint
of NordSüd Verlag AG, CH-8050 Zürich, Switzerland.
Originally published in 2023 in Poland under the title *Świętujemy cały rok!*
by Wydawnictwo "Nasza Księgarnia," Warszawa
Library of Congress Cataloging-in-Publication Data is available.
ISBN: 978-0-7358-4570-1
Printed by Neografia, Slovakia